Alexandra
Aisling
Pillo,
the Giant Chicken
The Adventures of Mr. Sharp

Cover created with wombo premium by dream.ai and postermy-wall premium.

Mr. Ward, a strange individual

It was a hot summer's day, with the blazing sun heating everything up like a hot oven. Only Mr. Liam Sharp was walking down the street, extremely proud, with a shabby old pair of skates hanging around his neck. People stopped and stared at him, because you wouldn't expect to see such a sight in the middle of summer. Not to mention the fact that he was dressed very smartly in his brown suit.

Judging by Mr. Sharp's physique, he was an extremely handsome man in his early thirties, with brown hair in a ponytail and a sparse, unevenly grown beard. Thin lips, green eyes, and an oval face with two small ears and a straight nose complete Mr. Sharp's image. If it weren't for the stubble, which looked like an unkempt lawn, you could swear you were looking at a teenager. He walked confidently, keeping his body straight and shrugging his shoulders slightly. He was a tall, well-built man, and Mr. Sharp's students fell in love with him, sending him all kinds of letters and notes, some of it downright naughty. He taught history at the local school, and his greatest passion was mythology.

There was also Aunt Clara, whom the relatives nicknamed Clarinette. For a while she had struggled to get rid of this impossible name, because she was an extremely important person, or so she thought. But her efforts to get rid of this cheeky analogy, which a cousin of hers had made after a summer vacation, had no effect. It was that vacation when Benjamin and Madison, who lived in Miami, came to her house for two weeks after arguing about every possible and impossible subject. Clara declared war on the cousins who had the audacity to rummage through her personal belongings, and Madison wore her clothes without asking. Clara protested several times, but her mother, Sarah, would not accept her complaints under any circumstances. Instead of bringing them closer together, Sarah made them fight even more, and for another week of the cousins' vacation, they did nothing but call each other names. But the two siblings, Ben and Madison, doubled down, and by the end of their vacation, Clara was none other than Cousin Clarinette.

Mr. Sharp's Aunt Clarinette was that impossible creature, all she could think about was cleaning and how to criticize him.

But now the aunt was on vacation in Banff. Mr. Sharp walked down the street and remembered how it all started. If the aunt wasn't home, was this the time to do something crazy? But what would that be? A strong wind blew in the morning as he opened the window and tried to drink his hot coffee on the porch. The wind smelled of winter and even though it was no less than 30 degrees Celsius outside, from that moment on, all he could think about was winter. Liam went back to his room and started to get his helmet, gloves and goggles out of the suitcase under his bed. Then he looked for his skates. But they were nowhere to be found; where could they be?

- Heaven forbid, Helios, the Titan with all his brothers and sisters if this isn't pure misfortune! By all the palace of Helios of gold, if there was not a brand-new pair of skates in that suitcase!

Soaked with sweat, Liam sat back in his chair, grabbed a soda from the fridge and began to think. Where could his skates be? For a moment, he considered calling his aunt and asking her, but his sensitive ear couldn't hear the shrill screams. Most likely, Aunt Clarinette was at the spa with one of her girlfriends, or rather, one of his new girlfriends. Wherever she went, this woman surrounded herself with dozens of friends whom she visited, or worse, who visited her at home. Actually, it's inappropriate to say her house, because he lived in the basement, in a one-room apartment attached to the lavish garage, while upstairs, on a whole level, Aunt Clarinette lived in luxury. Not only did this infamous creature have four bedrooms and plenty of space to live in, but when you least expected it, she would descend into Mr. Sharp's quarters and, without asking his permission, clean his room. That wasn't so bad, but when he needed something, he couldn't find it because his aunt had either moved it or thrown it away. Sure enough, she had given his brand-new skates to a friend who had a nephew who complained that his skates were too small.

Around half past ten, Liam Sharp decided to leave the house with the stated purpose of making an unscheduled visit to a large sporting goods store. He hurried to the closet and discovered that all of his clothes were either very dirty or almost very dirty. In other words, no one had washed them, and after several days of wearing them in the infernal heat, they were no longer wearable. Auntie's excessive care and compulsive behavior had its advantages. He had become accustomed to opening the closet door and seeing all the shirts ironed and laid out in stripes, all the trousers pressed and brushed, without a lint on them. In front of him, in all its glory, was his brown Sunday suit, the one Aunt Clarinette had bought him and made him wear when they both went to church.

He made a quick decision: he put on the suit and looked for a tie to match. Eventually he found a dull one, but that didn't matter because today he was going skating and breaking his addiction to listening to his aunt. Yes, he knew it was the 15th of July, but the goddess of luck would be with him. He started walking to calm his nerves, and the farther he got from the house, the freer he felt. He could tell that he felt a huge weight lifting from his shoulders, even though he had forgotten for days what it was like to listen to his aunt's endless chatter and her need to constantly exert control over him.

- So, what if I go skating? It's my problem, it's not a horror, it's the choice I made as an adult. You can go to the hot springs in Banff, if they have them, or the hot tub and drink wine with your new girlfriends! Yeah, you do that! And I'm free to skate like the truly independent young man that I am!

Liam realized he was talking to himself on the street, but no one was paying attention; most people probably thought the young man had a pair of headphones in his ear and was talking on the phone.

Outside the sporting goods store, his anger subsided. Sometimes it was good to have someone else looking out for him, thought the young man, who hadn't eaten a cooked meal in days and whose closet was a mess. But there was a line outside the store, and people were standing quietly in the hot sun. He got in line and struck up a conversation with an older gentleman who was puffing away every five seconds.

- No offense, Liam said, but why is everyone standing in line?

- That's absurd, sir, the man in front of him replied. It's outrageous. There are all kinds of discounts, sporting goods at 75 percent, some at 85 percent, so you realize why there's a line. But what I don't understand is why they won't let us in.

Liam regretted asking this rude gentleman, who touched his shoulder and chest several times while gesturing. The gentleman also spoke loudly and sometimes spat. So, Liam took a step back so he wouldn't be so close to the angry, loud man's big mouth. He tried not to continue the conversation, but it seemed to his new acquaintance that the conversation had just begun.

- I'm Mr. Ward, first name Kieran, but you call me Mr. Ward because I'm older than you, I might even be your father. Yes,

yes, young people today don't know what respect is. What's your name?

Liam wanted to tell him what his name was, but the great Zeus of Olympus, who was this chubby guy to interfere in his life?! Then he started making things up, like he did when Aunt Clarinette caught him doing something he wasn't supposed to.

- My name, Mr. Ward, is Agenor.

- What kind of a name is that? I've never heard such a name in my life, Mr. Ward scowled at Liam.

- It's a Greek name, my grandparents after my father are Greek, Liam was quick to lie.

- And what's your last name? the man became even more curious.

- Well... it's Sinon, Liam fumbled.

- Your name is Sinon? I've never heard of that! Strange, very strange! I mean, Mr. Agenor, you're with me now, and I'll take care of this mess.

- What do you mean, Mr. Ward? Liam marvels.

- So, no one knows when these 85% cuts start and end! I saw the workers and their families whispering to each other. They're all talking to each other, it's a real conspiracy.

Liam Sharp is getting more and more confused; it was clear that the man in front of him was out of his mind.

- I don't think it's a conspiracy, Liam mused more to himself than to the gentleman in front of him.

- Yes, it is a conspiracy, but you are young! I know, I was young once! Yes, it's a conspiracy and you don't believe it! I didn't believe it either, the fat man continued. Let me explain. I live no more and no less than six and a half minutes away from that store. So, I walk by all the time, I walk by every day, sir, and I don't know how the hell it happens, but I never get a discount. All these fantastic discounts start and end without customers like you and me being informed. Yesterday I came by and there was no one here, this morning I came by and what do you know? No discount! It's only now, when no one knew, that they started the discount. Luckily, I was passing by and saw it.

Liam was very annoyed by this character, who made him feel strangely anxious. He thought about leaving, but before he could make a clear decision, the clerk called out the next four people, so Mr. Ward grabbed him by the shoulder and pushed him into the store.

- Say thank you! That girl wanted to get in before you! It was you and me and the two skunk-smelling guys in front of us. We were in line to get in. And then you hesitated and someone else took your place. Sorry, I didn't ask, what are you looking for in the store?

While waiting, Mr. Ward moved his tongue very slowly, in a circular motion, between his teeth and gums, which Liam found totally disgusting.

- Well, I want a pair of skates, Liam replied.

- Skates you say you want, Mr. Ward mused, thinking and trying to visualize the winter goods aisle. "Okay, I know, upstairs, follow me up the escalator. Hurry, if you're lucky we'll find another pair of skates.

When they reached the winter gear section, the two of them started looking through several boxes of skates, but they were either children's or size 11 or 12.

- What are you wearing, Agenor? Mr. Ward stopped sweating from the effort of searching through the boxes.

- Number ten, Liam said, increasingly embarrassed by the man who had invaded his privacy and carried him around like his father.

- Yes, you wear the number ten, but on skates you know it's different, you must subtract another number, even half a number. All I could find was an eight. Come on, sit down here and see if your foot fits.

Mr. Ward had managed to attract the attention of all the employees and customers upstairs. He spoke loudly, in a hoarse voice; he was all over the place, gesticulating and randomly bumping into boxes or the shelf the boxes were on. Liam sat down in a chair and kicked off his shoes. He tried to get his foot in, but couldn't. Mr. Ward grabbed the skate and pulled the laces.

- That's the way to try, not with a tight lace. Come on, Mr. Ward urged him. Get your foot in the crystal conch, Cinderella!

A roar of laughter echoed through the sporting goods store. Despite Liam's best efforts, the foot wouldn't go into the skate.

- That's it, tough luck, sir, you can't say I didn't try, Mr. Ward
continued. Wait till I ask the salesmen if they have another
pair in stock.

Liam put on his shoes and thought about running away, but all
those dozens of stares kept him glued to his chair.

- Come on dad, dinner's ready, Liam called after making sure
Mr. Ward didn't hear him. Let's go home because Mother's
burning asparagus again.

Another roar of laughter swept through the store; people relaxed,
and everyone continued shopping. Liam congratulated himself on having such an inspiration. Obviously, it wasn't his lucky day. Agenor, the
great king of Tyre, couldn't find the skates. Poseidon, his father, was
apparently lost in the depths of the ocean, unable to answer his son
Agenor's calls. He began to smile. He, a professor of history and a lover
of Greek mythology and more, played such mind games.

But where could Mr. Ward be? Maybe now was the best time to
leave, but he figured that without skates his plan would never come to
fruition anyway. Maybe this would be a time to spend some more time
with the chubby guy he was starting to like a little. Besides, it was very
hot outside, and the air in the shop was the best remedy for a day when
everything around him was melting away. He waited for more than 20
minutes, during which time the floor of the sporting goods store emptied of shoppers.

- Serves them right, Mr. Ward puffed with satisfaction, holding a piece of paper like a diploma. I reached the store man-
ager! I complained to him, and here's the proof, this is my
complaint, it's a copy of my complaint. Let's see what else I
can buy.

The two of them went through the aisles, but the 85% off products had it written all over them: Out of stock.

- Well, you and me both, Mr. Agenor, we came for nothing. So, what do we do now?

- Mr. Ward, I was thinking of going home, skating is out of the question anyway. And I've got this crazy urge to scatter little bits of ice when I do a pirouette, or when I stop suddenly and the skates squeak on my feet.

- Too bad, sir, said the fellow, and he fell into thought. Hey, come on, I've got an idea, see if you don't like it. I live six and a half minutes from here, but if we pick up the pace, we'll be there in five. I think I have a pair of skates. They're not new, but if they fit, I'd be happy to give them to you. Come and try them on so you don't feel like you've come all this way for nothing.

Liam was surprised at how fast Mr. Ward was walking. He struggled to keep up, and by the time he was ready to strike up a conversation, the two of them were standing in front of a magnificent mansion, with a spacious courtyard and an entrance where two lions sat imperturbably.

- You like lions, Liam found himself saying.

- Oh, no, this is my Aunt Mary's house; she lives on a farm not far from here. I've had some trouble with my wife, I've had no place to live, and I can use this house, but I don't know for how long; at any moment my aunt may tell me to leave her house, or perhaps, in a gesture of goodwill, which is not like her, she may make a donation in my name and leave the house to me.

Liam thought about how lucky some people are. Aunt Clarinette would barely let him live in her little basement apartment; she wouldn't even let him up to her house when she was away. And this chubby fellow lived in luxury and opulence. The two lions didn't look like much from the street, but as Liam walked past them, he marveled at the detail and care with which they had been created, and the base read: "Baker Family Home".

The two entered the house. A large, spacious hallway lay ahead of them, and light streamed in from a window above the doorway that made one think of a cathedral. The house was elegantly decorated, and the staircase leading upstairs was adorned with a banister inlaid with gold ornaments. The chandelier in front of the staircase was imposing, with several arms like the tentacles of an octopus, adorned with electrical ornaments in the form of candles and crystals that sparkled and created a fairytale atmosphere. Liam thought to himself that this chandelier must have weighed about 200 pounds and thought about all the forces that had been used to get this chandelier into the position it was in now.

Liam marveled at how beautiful this house was. Aunt Clarinette had a house that could be considered a real palace, but this was something else. Mr. Ward's house had refinement and elegance, style and something extra. On the walls hung a series of old gold-framed paintings, depicting summer landscapes with nature dressed in vibrant colors.

Mr. Ward invited him into the upstairs study, and as he climbed the stairs, Liam carefully admired the decor, noting the beautiful long black velvet drapes, the old and probably extremely valuable furniture, and the large and extremely soft Persian rug underfoot.

MORE CURIOUS ABOUT the look of the whole house, Liam let himself be led through several bedrooms decorated in the same classical style. In front of them was a huge hall with marble floors and leather armchairs, and in the back was a library containing several thousand volumes, all covered in leather. To the right of the room was a white grand piano that had probably belonged to Aunt Mary and that Liam suspected no one had played in a long time. Next to this room was Mr. Ward's office, a small room with a dull desk and a laptop on it. The floor was the same white marble as the reception room upstairs, and the walls were wallpapered with a dark material he hadn't seen before.

- This is where I feel most at home, in my little room. I don't really like luxury, Mr. Ward said. "We have always been a simple family; perhaps many would have been glad to have a house like this left to them by an aunt whom I had hardly heard of in my childhood. I, however, would not have been so happy. This house, or whatever you want to call it, is more trouble than joy. But never mind, let's go to the garage.

Curious about what the garage might look like and what old cars might be in there, Liam turned in front of Mr. Ward and walked down the stairs to wait for him on the first level.

- This way, Mr. Ward said, leading him into a room that could hold at least three cars. But there was no sign of a car; the whole room was full of boxes in perfect order.

It seemed that in all that jumble of boxes on shelves, Mr. Ward knew exactly what and where they were. He quickly found his way around and pulled a box from a shelf on the right and found the pair of skates in the back.

- Mr. Agenor, here are the skates. These are number 9, actually you wear number 10 on your shoes and number 9 on your skates. Now, I want to tell you that those skates have a history. They have cost me over $18 million.

- What? All the work of Hercules! exclaimed Liam. You're joking, Mr. Ward.

- No, I'm not kidding. It's as true as it gets. Come into the living room, sit down, and I'll tell you the whole story from the beginning.

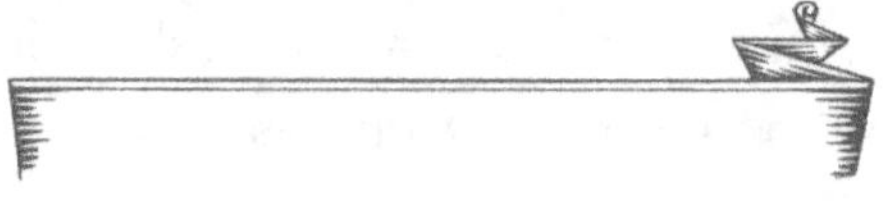

Squirrels vs. Sharks

Mr. Ward was extremely methodical when starting a story. Liam sat down on the spacious couch and felt that in addition to the coffee in the small cup he was sipping, a few more appetizers would do; he wouldn't mind if his hostess provided him with a hearty lunch. But Mr. Ward was extremely stingy when it came to offering anything. Next to the coffee, like two exhausted soldiers, sat two biscuits of dubious provenance, to say the least, and Liam, hungry as he was, had not touched them. They must have been there since Aunt Mary's last visit. In any case, this gentleman was rather odd; most likely Mr. Ward was hiding even more terrible secrets.

- What I want to say to you, Mr. Agenor... is that it rather bothers me to say your name, because each time I have to make an effort to remember it. Couldn't I use another name? Don't you have another name? What do your friends call you?

- Yes, Mr. Ward. Some of my acquaintances call me Liam, the young man blurted out, and for a moment he was sorry to have revealed himself, but Mr. Ward had been quite nice to him, and perhaps he deserved to know his real name at least.

- Well, Mr. Liam, that's more like it, and it's also the anagram of Peru's capital, Lima. I'll never forget it. I have to give you credit: even though I know what's in every nook and cranny of this house, I get terribly confused when it comes to names and people. To remember them, I have to associate them with all sorts of things. So, let's go back to the skates.

- You said those skates cost you $18 million, Liam said rather jokingly.

- At least that much money, if not more. I could've bought my own little palace and stopped worrying about Aunt Mary kicking me out! You don't think so, Mr. Liam, but what a chance! I was out buying cheap stuff at a garage sale. I know a couple of good places here in the neighborhood where people take all sorts of valuable stuff out of the garage and, guess what, sell it for pennies on the dollar. There's a lot of stuff you can find and resell yourself. One guy bought $20 worth of jewelry and when he took it to the jeweler, he valued it at over $350,000, real 20-carat diamonds. Not to mention you can find artwork, toys from the '50s, valuable books... even a pair of Nike Air Mag sneakers you can resell for $50,000.

I had a hunch: a small Chinese porcelain vase by the artist Qianlong; I had information that there might be one in the neighborhood that, if you managed to buy it at a bargain price, would resell for at least a few hundred thousand dollars. I was out of luck that day; there was no Chinese porcelain vase for sale. It was a Wednesday, and I never have any luck on Wednesdays. So, disappointed, I looked down at the small table in front of me and saw these ice skates. They weren't very good quality, but I felt that there was something special about these skates. I picked them up and was about to put them back on the table when I felt a shadowy man's eye on the back of my head. He had sunglasses and a handkerchief over his mouth; the man didn't look like he was from our neighborhood, and it seemed like he was there specifically for these skates. I grabbed the pair of skates and, without further negotiation, dropped $20 and left. At one point, when I turned my head, I thought I saw the man following me, so I got off the subway, went one way, then the other, changing lines until I was sure the man had lost track of me. I couldn't wait to get home and see what was wrong with those skates. I picked them up and studied them, and inside, written in marker, I found two names: Violet followed by three numbers: 4, 25 and 33 on one skate and Rufus followed by three more numbers on the other skate: 23, 41 and 44. The writing was pretty faded, I think it had been there for a couple of years, so it took me a day to piece together some of the almost-erased numbers. Tell me, Mr. Liam, am I boring you?

- Not at all, I find the subject more and more interesting. So, there were more numbers written on the skates. May I see them?

Mr. Ward opened one of the skates, and on the right side, next to the laces, you could see Rufus written, but the numbers were pretty faded. You couldn't see very well, but it looked like it said 23, 41 and 44.

- It could also be a 29, Liam thought to himself, but Mr. Ward didn't even hear him and continued the story with more enthusiasm.

- I didn't know what it meant. I thought of all sorts of combinations and had all sorts of theories. To avoid meeting the man who had been following me, I stayed in the house, but a week had passed, and I didn't know how to solve the mystery. Sometimes, when I couldn't sleep, I would turn on the small television in the bedroom. One night, when I couldn't fall asleep, I turned on the TV but forgot to program it to turn itself off. I woke up around 3am, it was night time and the TV was still on, I was between sleep and daydreaming when I heard my numbers, Mr. Liam, repeated on the TV. I jumped out of bed because I recognized them, they were Violet's and then Rufus's!

- I don't understand. What numbers were on the TV? Liam asked curiously.

- You wouldn't believe it! They were the lottery numbers, sir. If I'd found out earlier, I would have won $18,763,203 and 63 cents.

- By Cyclops' eye, if I can believe it!

- Yes, Mr. Liam. What a crooked business, all in your Cyclops Eye! It's driving me crazy. I didn't know what to do. I thought maybe I'd better get in touch with the man who followed me, he must have a clue about these skates, he must know something. Then I got scared and congratulated myself for walking away and not letting him follow me. I would have been happy with half the amount, what do I say half, I would have been happy with a million dollars! Can you imagine how such a fortune could slip through my fingers?!

- How did it happen, Mr. Ward? The writing has been there for years. Who could have written the winning numbers in a future lottery game? In Athena's wisdom, that's beyond a man's comprehension. Who could be Violet and Rufus? By what chance did the skates they wrote on come to you? Liam wondered.

- Don't think I haven't thought about all this, Mr. Ward breathed angrily, stroking his bushy beard. Here's what I've been thinking about these days. What if the man following me was none other than Rufus? What would you say now? What if I took the skates he wanted to buy? What if someone, somehow, gave Violette and Rufus the winning numbers and I got in the way and ruined the whole deal? What if they're looking for me now to get even? What do your gods say, Mr. Liam?

- By all the storms, lightning and thunder of Zeus, Mr. Ward! But I don't think you're right. You were just a shopper, like 20 or 30 others that afternoon. You just happened to take the skates that had been there for hours, and nobody wanted them. Maybe the man was following you for some other reason, maybe he was a treasure hunter, who knows?

- Anyway, Mr. Liam, please take the skates yourself. Now that I think about it, I don't really want them. I've had enough trouble with them. The most interesting thing was that it never occurred to me to think about the lottery numbers, and even if I did, I don't think I'd even play them out of curiosity. I didn't have a hunch this time, and I generally have a tremendous hunch, you know.

The conversation went on for a few more minutes, but the two touched on other topics related to the weather and sports. Liam finished his coffee but didn't touch his two biscuits, thank Mr. Ward and left with his skates tied around his neck.

- Whatever problems you have, Mr. Liam, don't hesitate to
come to me, I may be able to help, Mr. Ward called to him,
and Liam walked briskly away from his house.

Affected by the story he had just heard, Liam looked suspiciously
left and right, but no one followed the young man. He'd wasted enough
time, but the rink was close. On his way, the young man noticed that
the sidewalk was becoming increasingly crowded with young people,
and some of them had begun to wave at him.

- Hello Professor. Did you make it to the hockey game?

What hockey game was everyone talking about? Liam recognized
some of his students from the crowd.

Arriving at the arena, Liam didn't know what to believe anymore.
The usually empty parking lot, where kids used to ride their bikes while
parents discussed incredibly interesting topics and forgot to watch
their little ones, was now a cacophony of noise.

At some point, he found himself caught in the crowd and slowly
made his way to the front door. In the commotion, even Orpheus
would lose his lyre, given to him by his father, Apollo. But at the door,
the surprise was even greater! Several players from the hockey team
were waiting for him.

- Thank God you came! I left you several messages at home
and you didn't answer your cell phone.

He had left home hours ago, and his phone had been on silent
mode since he entered the sporting goods store. Then, with everything
that happened with Mr. Ward, the phone stayed that way. Liam passed
through security and, carried by the young people waiting for him,
reached the locker room of the Squirrels, who were about to face the
Sharks in an extremely challenging game. His students would be play-

ing the game that could qualify them for the fall season. The coach's face was flushed, and his whole body language showed that he felt lost, overwhelmed by the situation.

> - Mr. Professor, please, the coach said in a plaintive voice, these players need you!

Liam looked around, not understanding. What could he do in such a situation?

> - We need a motivational speech; the team needs encourage-ment. The Sharks seem unbeatable, but we can win, can't we?

In that moment, Liam felt for the first time what it was like to connect with an audience. He felt an electric shock that first tingled in his legs and then traveled up his spine to his brain. His mind became clear, and he felt his body like a volcano with words just waiting to erupt.

He climbed onto a chair in front of the Squirrels team and began to speak in a calm and solemn voice. He felt as if the universe had sent him to this place just to give this speech. The youngsters were captivated by his words from the very beginning.

> - Squirrels, I may not be the best person to encourage you, but you called me here, and I want to tell you that I am ex-tremely proud to speak in front of such a united and power-ful team! You are about to play an epic game. Maybe you're scared, maybe some of you are thinking about taking off your skates and running as far away from this place as you can. First and foremost, you need to understand that this is just a game. No one is asking you to do anything other than what you've been trained to do. No one is asking you to do anything but accept this challenge and give it your all! I am proud of you, and I believe in victory. I feel it and I believe

that you have earned your place in this game. You have a chance to play a game that people will remember. Go out on that ice and really show what you're made of, and no matter what happens, don't look down; look your opponents in the eye and show them that you're already celebrating the victory that will come. This game is not the end for you; this game is the beginning, and you cannot let your guard down. The Sharks are good, but you are better. They will try to take advantage of your weaknesses, but you are stronger. You are the Squirrels!

- Squirrels! Squirrels!

- The sharks are stuck in the water and cannot get out, but the squirrels are everywhere. They're in the trees, on the ground, jumping and running, and no one can catch them. The squirrels are unstoppable! Get on the field and play as a team, show the Sharks who's better! Play with honor and respect. Play for points. Let the Sharks run from the crazy Squirrels, let them run and hide in the deep waters, and on the ice, there should be nothing left but the Squirrels celebrating victory!

It was a beautiful speech. The team left the locker room like a pack of rabid squirrels, and the coach was in tears. Liam, a little unsure, asked him:

- How was it, Coach?

- Great, the coach said, choking back tears. Mr. Professor, I have one more request. The team only has one goalie, and I was thinking maybe you could step in as a backup goalie. What do you say?

- Well, I like to skate, but where's the backup?

- There was a mix-up, and the goalie is with his family at 6Flags. I haven't been able to reach him, and to make matters worse, our goalie has a stomachache. We can't afford to be without a goalie.

As Liam considered how to politely decline the coach's offer, he felt that surge of courage and madness from deep within.

- Yes, Coach. What do I have to do?

- Well, if you put on the backup goalie uniform, no one will recognize you. These rascals are about your size; we just need to put a hood over your head so that only your eyes are visible.

- Isn't that too obvious?

- Oh, not at all. Some goalies wear hoods because they sweat in that big helmet, and it sticks to their face.

- All right, Liam said, let's do it.

- Thank you for the speech and for agreeing to be our goalie, but please, total discretion. We don't want to risk being found out. I see you brought your skates.

- No problem; I have these skates with a rather peculiar history. Let's go, you go to the team, and I'll stay back to change.

- If I'm not asking too much...next to the locker room is a room where the janitor keeps his brooms and buckets for

cleaning. You can go in there and keep the key. No one needs
to know.

Liam found the room where the janitor kept his things to be quite
spacious. He first unlocked the door, made sure no one was in the hallway, and then quickly entered with all the equipment. Five minutes later, the Squirrels had a second goalie waiting patiently on the bench.

The game was a tough one, with both teams wanting to qualify, and
the tension was building even before the players took the ice. In the
first period, the Sharks weren't intimidated by the courage of the Squirrels, who seemed to soar on their skates after Liam's golden speech. The
Squirrels scored a quick goal against their opponents, but the Sharks
bounced back and tied the game.

Both teams began to play strategically, and the first period ended
with a tight score and no additional goals. The Sharks were the better
team on the ice, but the Squirrels weren't going to back down. In the
second period, the Squirrels scored an own goal and the magic seemed
to disappear. The Sharks dominated the field and scored two more
goals, weakening the Squirrels' defense.

At the end of the second period, the Squirrels' goalie rushed to the
bathroom and remained there, apparently overcome with emotion.

- Mr. Professor, the coach said, please don't let us down. Get
on the field and play goalie. I know it's 4-1, but maybe we
still have a chance. We'll pray to Zeus, the coach said uncon-
vincingly, trying to persuade Liam.

By some miracle, Liam didn't even know he was in the goal. The
Sharks were already feeling confident, but after a few attacks, Liam
heroically defended the goal. When a puck hit him hard in the helmet,
Liam was furious. The opponent had done it gratuitously, not aiming
at the goal, but at his helmet. If he had intended to defend the best he

could up to that point, from that moment on his only goal was to win the game.

Interestingly, he felt that surge again, that extraordinary strength. If he thought about the past, he would usually be afraid of new and challenging situations, but now it was the opposite. Adrenaline surged through his body, and he felt incredibly combative. Taking advantage of the numerical advantage, as a Shark had just been sent to the bench, Liam took the puck, dribbled past a couple of players, and from the middle of the rink, he fired the puck into the back of the net with no one looking. It was unbelievable.

The game continued. The Sharks gave up their superior attitude and began to take the final period seriously, but it was too late. Liam was everywhere, in goal and on defense, coordinating the Squirrels, who had scored a beautiful goal. In this infernal tension, the Sharks pulled their goalie and added an attacker to go all out on the attack. However, it seemed to be a mistake as Liam, with an agility and precision that surprised even himself, went past the Sharks goal to tie the game.

Everyone thought the game would go into overtime, but in the last 40 seconds Liam scored two more points. The game was won by the team's goalie. This had never happened before! All the spectators were on their feet, applauding wildly. The Squirrels' victory was truly an extraordinary event, and both the crowd and the press in attendance rushed to the bench to congratulate and interview the amazing goalie.

In the midst of the commotion, the coach managed to call out to Liam:

- Mr. Professor, run! Hide in the room where you changed and don't come out!

Flanked by three Squirrels players, Liam began to run down the hallway. When he reached the front of the janitor's storage room, Liam dropped to his knees and opened the door, and the three players positioned themselves to block the view of those at the end of the corridor. With some effort and drenched in sweat, Liam managed to enter the janitor's storage room, realizing that the key had been left on the other side, but one of the Squirrels players closed the door and yelled:

- I'm coming to unlock it for you, Mr. Professor, don't worry!

For a second, Liam felt a shiver of fear run down his spine. He had the feeling that someone else was with him. But who could it be? He took off his gloves and felt his phone hanging from his neck by a special cord. He opened it, intending to use the phone's flashlight to illuminate the room, but his phone kept receiving notifications. He tapped on one, and it was a live stream from the stadium. A well-known journalist, Elora Roslyn, was broadcasting the entire game live from her phone, and now everyone was wondering where the miracle goalie was who had turned the game around for the Squirrels. Liam was stunned when he saw that over 2.5 million users were watching the journalist's broadcast. How was he going to get out of this? If they were caught cheating, the Squirrels would face disqualification and he could even get fired.

Liam was sweating profusely and was about to take off his hockey helmet when, in the light of the phone screen, he saw a figure approaching him, nearly six feet tall and covered in yellow feathers: it looked like a giant bird. Liam screamed as loud as he could. The bird got scared and pecked him on the head. Luckily, Liam hadn't managed to take off his helmet! But the emotional shock and the peck sent Liam into the world of Morpheus. Was this bird-like creature a winged spirit that created dreams for humans? But this was probably a dream created by Phobetor; it was a terrifying dream.

Elora Roslyn

Elora Roslyn was already known throughout the city for her incendiary articles in the city's most widely read newspaper. It was no wonder that many were afraid of her, even when trying to call them on the phone. She had always been the class geek, and she had suffered greatly for it. Nobody liked her, and boys were intimidated by a girl who was much smarter than them, preferring the company of girls who were only interested in fashion and gossip.

In school, Elora had never had any friends, and ten years later, the situation hadn't changed much. Good grades had been replaced by well-written articles and journalism awards, the envy of her peers. Her photo on the lobby wall with the most coveted local award was enough to create a wave of jealousy. There was also a secret that Elora held, one that would completely change the course of events, but we would probably find out about it later.

- Good morning, Miss Elora, was the gentle voice of Mr. Eric Collins, the only one who cared for her in this media institution. You have an envelope to pick up from me, he whispered so no one else could hear.

- Good morning, Mr. Eric. I'll pick it up later, she replied in the same hushed tone. This meant that one of her secret sources had left extremely important information.

She trusted only Mr. Collins, and when there were other employees in the hallway, Elora would go downstairs and bring Mr. Collins a coffee, who would seize the moment to slip the envelope without anyone suspecting anything.

Elora had to go to a hockey game; it wasn't her style, but a colleague had asked for her help because he was getting married. Yes, it was unexpected, a kind of love at first sight. That feeling that grabs you and holds you for exactly 24 hours, after which you wonder why no one stopped you. Well, no one tried to stop Ted because he was a rather unbearable character with his direct jokes that would hit you and change your mood when you least expected it. On the contrary, everyone encouraged him and wished him luck. The truth is that the best marriages are the ones that happen quickly, and if they last, it's called hitting the jackpot. In a society where divorce rates are on the rise, Elora wasn't interested in relationships, and her time was precious because she always had the highest aspirations.

The hockey game itself was no event. In fact, one of the teams had been disqualified and couldn't participate in the fall championships, so two other teams that hadn't qualified were playing now, and the winner would play in the local league. It was beneath her as an award-winning journalist to attend and write about such banality! The Squirrels big game, who in the world would name a hockey team "The Squirrels"? But Mr. Collins had an envelope for her, so she went to the top floor, where they make the best coffee in town. She ordered an espresso con panna for herself and a ristretto for him, then went downstairs for lunch, and the two of them went out into the courtyard. They chatted for a few minutes about the most mundane things, and then Mr. Collins excused himself and left, because someone was waiting for him in the lobby of the institution. Without anyone noticing, there was a small letter on the bench, which Elora quickly grabbed when no one was around and put it in her bag. This anonymous source was about to provide another piece of first-rate information for her article. This source knew about the events before they happened. It was very strange and provocative.

At some point, Elora woke up one morning with the idea of conducting an investigation into this secret source. She had written a detailed plan and thought about putting it into action; she had resources and was a good investigative journalist. But after five minutes, she changed her mind, abandoned the plan, and decided it was better not to complicate things. The next day, Mr. Collins left a small letter on her desk. Elora opened it while her colleagues were at lunch and couldn't believe what she read: "Don't try to find me again; you're making a big mistake!" How could The Source know that she intended to seek and find it?

Once home, Elora checked every corner of her house; she looked everywhere for a surveillance camera but couldn't find one. She found the discarded pieces of paper in the trash and thought that no one had been in her apartment. This was incredibly strange! It seemed that The Source had other ways of finding out things.

After this incident, The Source didn't contact her for several weeks. Elora wrote a disguised article for young ladies about good manners and how to properly apologize. The article appeared on the front page of the newspaper, and after this article, the Source contacted her again. She had learned her lesson, and it seemed that as long as the Source delivered valuable information, she didn't care who it was.

Elora walked out into the street and got into the car parked a few blocks away. She was tempted to open the envelope in the courtyard, but she refrained. She had learned to follow a strict protocol, especially because she didn't want to lose The Source's trust again.

She opened it and read: "The Squirrels win! Keep an eye on their backup goalie." And as a signature, the same Q. Who was Q? Who could it be, and how did The Source get all this information? What could this mean? Who was the Squirrels' backup goalie, and why was he so important? The Source had never given false information. Elora returned to her office and fed the letter into the high-powered shredder, where the information was irretrievably lost in the tiny shreds of paper.

The journalist searched for the website of the Squirrels, the hockey team of a college with not too many athletic ambitions. Unfortunately, she couldn't find anything except some information about admissions and internal rules and regulations. Her only chance to learn more was to visit the college and hope that the coach was still there, trying to load the players' equipment onto the team bus.

Her intuition worked, and Elora found the coach; small, thin, and sweating in front of the college, the coach was surrounded by several bags of equipment and giving orders to several rowdy students, senior members of the hockey team. Elora walked straight up to the bus, and as the coach nervously turned around because he was running late, he stopped in astonishment to see the charming young journalist, armed with a recorder, pointing at him.

- I'm from the local press, my name is Elora, and I'd like to do
a quick interview with you about tonight's game, she said.

The coach swallowed hard a few times, yelled at the rowdies to load all the equipment, and then relaxed, his face breaking into a broad smile.

- Of course, even though we're a bit pressed for time, I can
spare a few words.

Elora had that effect on most men. Her large, dark eyes and stag's gaze disarmed even the most stubborn opponent. She had a charisma that couldn't be ignored, a way of speaking that started out neutral and then turned into enthusiasm. She smiled during pauses in the conversation and looked them directly in the eye, making them feel both embarrassed and extremely important.

- I'd like to know what your goals are for the new season if you qualify, and which players you're counting on tonight; I'd like to know their names, too. You know, we at the newspaper are quite accurate, unlike others who have mixed up team players, although it has happened before. Not to me, but to my colleagues in the press.

- Of course, the coach replied, if you can take a picture with your phone, here's the list of players; I hope you'll use it.

- I don't understand what you mean, Elora wondered.

- I mean to write an article about us, the winners, because nobody writes about the losers anymore.

- Oh yes, definitely, I hope you have a memorable game.

The list was now on her phone; she returned to her office and looked up the reserve goalkeeper. Through some cross-referencing, she found the phone number and address in just a few minutes. She called the home phone, but no one answered. She got in her car and within 30 minutes she was on the beautiful lawn of the famous Dylan "The Brick Wall" Thompson. However, it appeared that the family car was not in the driveway. Fortunately, a neighbor recognized her and quickly filled her in on what had happened. The Thompson family was not home because they had all left town, including backup goalie Dylan.

Something was suspicious; if the game was only a few hours away, how could the backup goalie be gone? There were only two and a half hours until the game. She hurried to the stadium to watch the game from there, armed with two spy cameras, a small monitor, and a charged cell phone. Tonight, she was going to solve the mystery of the reserve goalkeeper. Then she had a feeling of déjà vu. Damn all these sensations, as if things had happened before!

As Elora prepares for what could be an extraordinary, but also scandalous article, our narrative thread shifts to another person, and her story begins like this:

Once upon a time, there was an extremely curious girl, but we won't reveal her real name for now, who grew up in a home filled with love, with parents who surrounded her with care and supported her in all her endeavors. Because she had a desire to know, she bombarded the adults with all kinds of questions and wouldn't stop until she received answers to all her inquiries. She began to keep a diary of questions. How big is the moon? How many people live in our town? How much water does a guinea pig drink in a day? Why is the sky blue? Why don't fish make sounds? After several months, the girl changed her questions and started writing in her journal: What if the moon were as big as the sun? What if the sky wasn't blue? What if fish could talk? And from each answer came a wonderful story, each beginning with: Once upon a time.

She kept growing, and her universe kept getting bigger, and to understand it, she started traveling. Because she was so good at what she did, a prestigious newspaper hired her to write stories from these travels. Wherever she went, the girl created fantastic stories. One evening, while staying in a hotel after attending a technology conference, she wondered what it would be like if a fantastic creature appeared in her room, and the thought led her to think of a lemur. She was about to fall asleep when a cute and shy lemur suddenly appeared in front of her.

- Who are you? the girl asked, surprised by her companion.

- I am a lemur from Madagascar.

- And how can you speak? the girl wondered.

- I can only speak to those of my own kind, but in this dream, you can ask me anything, and I will answer you.

- Tell me about you and your family.

- We are several brothers and sisters, the lemur began, approaching the girl, and she began to stroke his soft fur with her fingertips. She could hear the rustling of leaves from the wind near their home, the sun shining brightly, and the sounds of other animals in the jungle. "We like to play, but we have to be careful of predators; we have to be smart to survive, the lemur continued. Animals are a danger that every lemur knows how to avoid. But once the little lemur met a group of hunters looking for an elephant bird's nest. More stories followed, and eventually the alarm clock rang. But everything felt so real, and she could still feel the soft fur of the lemur under her hand.

Since then, the girl continued to explore the world in this way, and each morning she woke up with a new story, which she faithfully recorded in her journal. However beautiful the stories were, she felt that something was missing, and she wanted to share her thoughts and feelings with the real world. She wasn't thinking about a romantic relationship because such interactions always ended badly, especially for a journalist who had to get out of bed at any hour to write a news story. She wanted more than that; she wanted a real friend, someone close, like family. But other than her parents, she had no one, so all she had left were the trips she took in her dreams that seemed so real.

When she arrived at the stadium, a security guard recognized Elora and let her in. Unfortunately, she didn't know which of the two locker rooms the Squirrels team would be using, so she took some sheets of paper, crumpled them up, and placed the two hidden cameras inside so they would blend in. She placed one of the cameras on a shelf in one locker room, among other discarded boxes and wrappers. The second one was more difficult, but with her characteristic ingenuity, she found a perfect angle near the trash can. Elora walked over to the stands and checked the monitor, which was transmitting video and audio perfectly. She put on an earpiece to listen to the sound recorded by the cameras and began to lose herself in the scenery. The spectators began to take their seats, preparing for the pregame ice show: 20 minutes of cheerleading. She went to the shop in the lobby and bought a huge hat and a pair of glasses; disguised, Elora sat down next to the Squirrels bench.

A few minutes after entering the locker room, the Sharks started pushing each other like childish kids, and somehow one of them hit the basket and blocked the camera. Anyway, the source was talking about the Squirrels team, so the journalist still had a working camera.

The crowd was slowly filling the arena, and the game was about to start. At that moment, her attention was drawn to a figure entering the Squirrels' locker room. He was a tall man, and the camera on the shelf managed to capture him quite well. There was a lot of noise, but at some point, it became quiet, and Elora could hear an extraordinary motivational speech, after which the Squirrels team courageously left the locker room.

She was about to turn off the camera, but at the last second, she caught a conversation of the utmost importance that was about to lead to a huge scandal. The man making the speech was none other than Liam Sharp, a history teacher at a local school. The coach had asked him to take the field in place of the reserve goalkeeper. So, the Source was right again; how could they have known all this in advance?! Elora, who witnessed the discussion, heard the coach asking the teacher to be the substitute goalkeeper. It was unexpected, neither of them knew what was going to happen half an hour ago, and yet the note Mr. Collins gave her a few hours ago said not to take the Squirrels' backup goalie out of her mind for a moment. It was completely insane that The Source knew this before the event had a chance to happen.

After a few minutes, the Squirrels' backup goalie appeared on the bench. No one paid any attention to him, but with her highly developed powers of observation, she immediately recognized the history teacher. The Squirrels wanted to cheat, but she wasn't going to let them.

First, she needed proof, so she took out her phone and started a live stream on the main video-sharing platform.

She watched the game: the Sharks had scored several times, and despite the teacher's speech, the Squirrels were on the verge of defeat. But in the final period, the reserve goalkeeper entered the game. And then two miracles happened. First, the live stream of the hockey game had more than two million viewers, and the number was growing. In her best live streams, Elora could only get a few hundred viewers. But the most incredible thing was that the backup goalie, aka Professor Liam Sharp, managed to turn the game around and win the game all by himself!

The team headed back to the locker rooms, and Elora made her way to the Squirrels' locker room to say goodbye to those who had watched her live. After the broadcast ended, she started to film the way to the Squirrels' locker room with her cell phone, and this would be the proof that they had cheated. At the end of the corridor, she saw Liam Sharp running, surrounded by three Squirrels players. Just before the locker room, however, was the janitor's room, which one of the young men opened, and she saw Liam enter the room. The players had barely closed the door with the key when Elora, with her phone pointed at the young men, threatened them:

- You're live, open the door now, I'm from the press, Elora Roslyn is my name.

Reluctantly, one of the Squirrels players opened the door. With her cell phone in hand to record any movement in the janitor's room, she turned on the light and... surprise! There was no one in the room.

Who is Pillo?

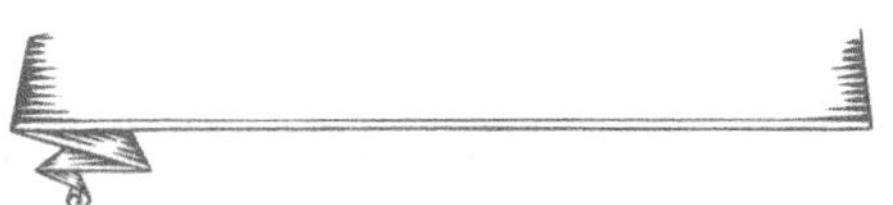

We have to admit that no one in Liam's position wouldn't have known what to believe when he woke up. It all seemed too impossible to be true. He had played a perfect game and scored the goals that qualified the Squirrels for the big leagues; he had run away from the cheering crowd; he had been followed online by more than 2.5 million hockey fans; and he had been hiding in the janitor's closet when a giant bird had hit him on the head with its beak. Most likely it was a person dressed like that, or maybe it was an ostrich stuck in the same room with him; who knew?

Liam struggled to get up and felt like he was sore all over, like after an intense day at the gym. The room was still dark.

- Hey, is anybody there? If you're going to hit me again, please let me know so I can keep my helmet on, just like Perseus. Who is Perseus, you ask? Well, that's easy; he's the mythological hero who killed Medusa.

Liam finally found his phone and turned on the flashlight again, and in front of him he saw something he had never imagined: a gigantic chick, over two meters tall and over 200 kilograms, with yellow and soft feathers, a yellow beak, and two huge, gentle eyes. As Liam looked into the giant chick's eyes, all fear left him, for those eyes radiated calm and kindness.

Liam stood up and turned on the light from the wall switch. The giant chick recoiled and cowered in the corner of the room.

- Don't be afraid, little one, no one's going to hurt you. But the chick kept trembling, as big as it was. Come on, don't be afraid. Liam approached the giant chick and began to stroke its back, and at that moment the chick made a sound like a child's whimper and calmed down.

Looking around, Liam was surprised to see that the entire caretaker's room was in total disarray. The chick had probably gotten scared and flapped around, knocking over buckets, brooms and cleaning supplies, but that was the least of Liam's problems. How was he going to get out of here, and what explanations was he going to give after the hockey game? There was also that journalist, Miss Roslyn, who once she got a story, wouldn't let go until she uncovered the truth. If she had broadcast the hockey game and millions of people around the world had seen it, then she was definitely following the story.

Finally, Liam remembered that the three players had locked him in that janitor's room, and he didn't have the key.

- What do we do, are we stuck here?
- Pillo, Piiiiiiiii, Hmmmm, Hmmmmm!

Liam was speechless and realized that something was bothering him. He was still wearing the hockey goalie helmet, which was not comfortable at all. He felt like he couldn't breathe, and he was sweating too much in the goalie suit. But he forgot all that because the giant chick had just talked to him. It had at least articulated a word.

- Is your name Pillo?
- Pillo, aaaaaaaaaa!
- What are you doing here, Pillo?
- Pillo!

It seemed that this was the only word the chick could say. It wasn't unusual for some birds to talk. Liam remembered the neighbors' parrot that sat on their patio during the summer and terrorized him on vacation days by waking him up at 6 in the morning.

Who could this chick be? Liam had no idea. Without hesitation, he began to undress and realized that his clothes were in the Squirrels' locker room. He found a janitor's robe and some plastic slippers and dressed up. He was able to leave the room without anyone laughing at him; the hood that had hidden his face became a hat, and so disguised, he tried to see if the door was still locked. Surprisingly, the door was open and there was no one in the hallway. It was completely silent, and Liam guessed that it must have been a few hours since he had hidden here, and all the onlookers had gone home.

Lost in these thoughts, Liam was moving away from the janitor's room when he heard a voice that tore at his soul.

- Pillo, Pillo!

What was he going to do with this giant chick? How could he take it to the streets? At the same time, there was something special about the giant chick, and against all logic, Liam felt that he had to take the chick with him. He felt that excitement again, the one he felt when he gave a speech to the Squirrels team and when he scored the winning goals.

Liam walked slowly down the corridor, instructing the chick to follow him quietly. The chick seemed to understand that Liam was going to take it with him and cooperated fully. He found no clothes in the locker room, so he had to stay in the robe. The doors to the hockey arena were still open and Liam approached the security guard and smiled. He looked up from his phone, smiled back and let them pass.

- May Apollo, the god of prophecy, inspire us and help us find a place where I can hide you.

Liam felt downright ridiculous in a tank top and underwear over which he wore the janitor's robe, plastic slippers on his feet, and a hood that he turned into a hat. He walked slowly, followed by a giant chick. But to his amazement, no one seemed to care about them. Some people stopped and smiled as they walked by, as if Liam was walking a dog, not a six-foot chick. But when he reached the bus stop, Liam was amazed at the reaction of the driver, who lowered the bus to make it easier for Pillo to get on.

- Half fare for the little one, just so you know, the driver said, closing the doors and continuing on his way.

- By all the gods of Olympus and those of Asgard, if something extremely strange doesn't happen right now! Am I dreaming, did I not wake up after Pillo hit me with his beak in the hockey helmet? How is that possible?

Liam expected the world to scream in horror and run away from Pillo, but everyone, without exception, behaved extremely naturally, as if it was perfectly normal to get on a bus with a 200-kilogram chick. Probably everyone thought that Pillo was a mascot. That might explain the relaxed attitude of the people around them. In addition, two young lovers stood up and offered their seats to Pillo, who now looked curiously out the window.

Everything was calm, unusually calm. Occasionally a traveler would approach and take a selfie with Pillo, and he was extremely excited about it. Liam found it amusing that everyone called him "Little One"; somehow the name suited him, because beyond his massive appearance, Pillo was just a chick, a child.

Eventually they got off the bus, but not before the driver and passengers laughed and applauded Pillo, who was at the height of happiness. So far, it seemed that the gods had protected him, but what was he going to do next with this chick? Fortunately, Aunt Clarinette had been away in Banff for a week, but he still had to sneak into the house without the neighbors seeing him and reporting to his aunt, as they always did. Those neighbors were extremely nosy, for one thing, because they interfered in his life, and for another, they had nothing else to do, no job, no occupation, because they were always at the window and didn't miss any of Liam's movements. "And to think," Liam said to himself, "that all this happened because of those damn new skates that Auntie gave or threw away!" At that moment, Liam remembered the skates and realized that he had left them in the janitor's room. He should have taken them and kept them, but now it was impossible to go back to the hockey rink with Pillo.

Nothing had prepared Liam for what was about to happen! Standing outside his house, Liam saw people going in and out; there was a butler at the door and a big party going on inside. Maybe Aunt Clarinette had returned without telling him, but how could that happen? The house had an extra floor!

Liam stared absentmindedly for over a minute until the shock wore off a bit; he saw well, and he wasn't hallucinating. In the basement was the garage next to his small apartment, but above it wasn't just one level where his aunt lived, but two, plus the attic. At that moment, Liam didn't want to know anymore and rushed to his apartment door, which he quickly opened and sat down at his desk in front of the laptop. He started to search the internet for specific information because things had already gone completely haywire. Finally, Pillo entered the house and sat down on the sofa. Liam first checked the date, and it was indeed July 1st. Furthermore, all the information he looked up matched what he already knew. At some point, however, wrinkles appeared on Liam's forehead, a sign that things were getting quite confusing. He searched for the hockey game and found a news article stating that the Squirrels and Sharks game would take place in 2 weeks, on July 15th. How was that possible?

Meanwhile, Pillo found some cookie bags in the pantry and started eating, a sign that he was extremely hungry. In the kitchen, he ate the apples and bananas that were in a fruit basket and then managed to open the refrigerator and tactfully started eating everything he found, but Liam ignored him. Liam searched for the recording of the journalist's live feed, but it was nowhere to be found. Instead, she had filmed and posted on her account a group of seniors playing bocce in the park.

Liam then searched online maps and navigated to his street, and the pictures showed Aunt Clarinette's house with two stories and an attic instead of one story and an attic. He changed the date, and in several posts from different years, the house looked identical to what he had seen earlier.

- This is not the world I woke up to this morning. By the hammer of Hephaestus, I must be in another universe now!

But Liam didn't get a chance to say more when he heard the sound of footsteps, Aunt Clarinette descending on his apartment. In a second, Liam got up from his desk, grabbed Pillo, and locked him in the bathroom just in time. On the doorstep, he found his aunt dressed in an elegant gown, with a well-coiffed hairdo and a fan in her hand.

- Where have you been, Liam? Why don't you answer your phone? Why are you dressed like that? We've been waiting for you for over an hour! Even that girl, the journalist Elora, wants to interview you. Come in 5 minutes, okay?

- Yes, Aunt, I'll be right there.

That was all Liam could say. After Aunt Clarinette closed the door, Liam rushed to the closet to change out of the janitor's robe he was still wearing. Instead of his usual brown suit, he found perfectly pressed tails and a pair of shiny black shoes. These clothes weren't his, reinforcing his belief that this was an alternate universe.

Liam dressed and went to the bathroom to comb his hair and freshen up. He was so engrossed in his new discovery that he forgot about the chick he had locked in the bathroom. However, Pillo didn't seem to care and drank all the water from the toilet. After eating everything in the fridge, the giant chick got thirsty.

> - Pillo, stay here and wait for me, okay? Don't move! I'm going upstairs to solve the mystery and see where we are, little one.

> - Pillo, lo lo lo! The chick replied, and Liam took that "lo" as a kind of "yes".

He left the window open in the living room and the bathroom door open so the chicken wouldn't suffocate, but he locked the apartment with the key, just in case, and because he thought a lot of crazy things had happened anyway, and he didn't feel like looking for Pillo in the city at night.

Aunt Clarinette's apartment wasn't much different from the one she knew, but what seemed different was the wealth that was everywhere. From the gold-inlaid wooden staircase to the paintings, which Liam estimated to be worth at least as much as an entire house. If he had once considered his aunt rich, now this house was too much for one person. He approached his aunt, surrounded by middle-aged people and a girl he found extremely attractive from the first moment.

> - Meet my nephew, a university assistant, a young man with great potential.

That was the height of everything! So, he wasn't a teacher at the neighborhood school anymore; he was now an assistant at the university! "By the wings of Hermes, if this universe isn't crazy!" Liam thought with a smile.

Liam didn't pay much attention to the others, exchanged a brief greeting, and when he reached the journalist, he felt his hands were icy. He felt a touch that confused him, a warm and soft hand. The sensation traveled down his spine to the back of his neck. There was something about this journalist that he couldn't quite put his finger on, but there was something strange about him.

- Pleased to meet you. I don't read much press, but I've heard about you and I'm glad to finally meet you. Liam Sharp is my name.

- I am Elora, the girl said with a cold voice, a stark contrast to the warmth of her body. Tell me, Mr. Liam, what do you teach university students?

Here Liam didn't know what to say. If he were in another universe, he could teach anything from cell biology, gastronomy, physical education to quantum mechanics. But the question was so direct that he couldn't avoid it.

- Liam teaches Ancient History, or to be more precise, he's getting his Ph.D. in Ancient Gods. Not to brag, but I gave him the first book on mythology, Aunt Clarinette said.

Liam breathed a sigh of relief, first because the wise Athena had made his double in this universe share the same passion as him, the one from the other universe, and second because Aunt Clarinette had saved him from an embarrassing situation he couldn't escape without raising more questions that would lead to more awkward situations. From now on, he could talk about gods and goddesses for two days straight, and no one could stop him.

- Thank you, dear aunt, I don't know what I would have done without your support. I've loved history since I was little.

- No, Liam, it wasn't like that at first. You should know, Miss, that this young man here wanted to be a mathematician! Then, whispering conspiratorially to the journalist, Aunt Clarinette continued, But I wouldn't let him. Then she continued loudly so that other guests at the party could hear. There are mathematicians in our town, but a mythologist, excuse me, there's only one! The journalist wants to interview you, but I asked her to stay until the end, after the guests have left.

- Tell me, Mr. Liam, do you like sports?

- I prefer team sports, Miss.

- Very interesting. I like to play bocce; when was the last time you played bocce?

Liam looked totally surprised! Where did this journalist come up with such specific questions? Bocce was a sport with metal balls, nonsense.

- I don't like that game; I don't think I've ever played it. Then the young man regretted his answer because his gesture could be interpreted as rudeness. He really needed to talk to the journalist and be more approachable.

- Liam is completely dedicated to his studies, Miss Elora. He's a nephew any aunt would want.

He lived to see it: Aunt Clarinette praising him! Besides these good things, Liam kept thinking about what to do with the giant chick who knew what he was doing in the bathroom, if there was still a bathroom and he hadn't panicked and destroyed everything in it. But he couldn't leave until he talked to the journalist. Liam wanted to see if she knew something and if she knew what she knew, and secondly, the meeting with this creature with a hot body but a cold voice like a robot intrigued him enormously. Every time he thought about what had happened in the last few hours, his mind made an enormous effort to adapt to the new information. Is it possible to go to another universe? But what happened to the original universe he left? Where is Liam Sharp from that universe? Why aren't there two Liams if he came from another universe? Shouldn't there be some sort of paradox if the same entity exists twice in the same universe? What is Pillo's role in this whole equation?

Liam tried to approach Elora and talk to her, but she seemed very engrossed in various other discussions. His concern for Pillo was growing, and he kept putting off the time to leave the party. As he approached the group where Elora was, his attention was drawn to the subject of hockey. Two gentlemen, whom the journalist seemed to have known for a long time, were intensely discussing a team that had just been eliminated, and now two other teams were about to play, with the winner advancing to the local league in the fall. "What a coincidence," Liam thought, knowing the story quite well. He was sitting on a sofa just a few feet away from the three of them who were having a heated discussion. It was only on the couch that the young man realized that his feet were terribly sore: he had really played the hockey game. The conversation went nowhere, and Liam wanted to get up and go down to his apartment; he was tired, and the journalist seemed to ignore him. Suddenly, he lost interest in her and called her a snob, but a beautiful snob.

Admiring his aunt's beautiful furniture in this universe, Liam congratulated himself for still being seated, because Elora said something that would have made him dizzy and fall to the floor.

- Let's consider a hypothesis that may seem downright impossible. Imagine, gentlemen, what it would be like if a team was led by one of the two in the first two halves, and the reserve goalkeeper tied the game in the last half and scored the goals that won the game. A simple reserve goalkeeper could change the fate of an entire team! The two men laughed out loud.

- Such a thing, dear Elora, has a chance of 1 in 14 million. It's practically impossible for such a thing to happen! Then the three continued laughing.

Liam got up and left in a hurry; what he heard made his whole body shake. Arriving at his apartment, he checked on Pillo:

- Hey, little one, are you okay? I haven't been gone long, and I hope you didn't do anything stupid here!" But the giant chick was sleeping in the bathtub with a happy chick face. Liam thought he might be cold and grabbed a blanket to cover him. He turned off the light, closed everything and went to bed.

"This journalist knows more than I thought! She seems to be an extremely dangerous being. With her impersonal and distant voice! I must avoid her as much as possible, oh Eris, great goddess of discord!" And with that thought, Liam fell asleep, overwhelmed by the fatigue and emotions of the day.

Another Liam

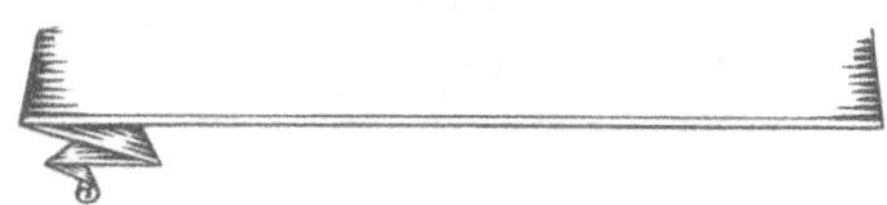

Once upon a time, a well-known journalist attended a hockey game between two relatively unknown teams. A reliable source provided her with one of the most scandalous stories in the press. What could have happened that was so unusual? Nothing foreshadowed the fact that a professor would take the place of the reserve goalkeeper, and not only that, but also win the game with a score of 4-6, scoring no less than 5 goals in a single period! The journalist filmed everything live, and the game was watched by over 2.5 million viewers worldwide. She wanted to expose everything and catch the impostor, but the utility room where the professor was hiding was empty. Liam Sharp, the history professor, had vanished without a trace.

Elora awoke suddenly with a feeling of frustration. In her dream, she had heard her father telling her to get ready for school. It was still a strange dream, but it seemed very real. In addition to her father's voice still ringing in her ears, Elora felt the excitement and adrenaline of the match. One name stuck in her mind: Liam Sharp, the trickster of her dream. She checked to see if there was a hockey game scheduled, and indeed there was, but it was two weeks away. So, there was a chance that things would happen exactly as she had dreamed. She had to start investigating as soon as possible. Who was this Mr. Sharp? Where did he live and at which school did he teach history? Elora, on her second cup of coffee of the day, found no high school teacher by that name. It was strange. Perhaps Mr. Sharp had indeed hidden his identity. Or perhaps he had assumed a false identity? More questions overwhelmed her. Her journalist's mind could not accept simple explanations.

Finally, Elora found a Liam Sharp, wrote down his address and went to his home. She didn't have much to do today; she had to write an article about a bocce championship. She could do that without going there, but professional ethics demanded that she spend at least a few minutes on the bocce field, talk to at least one person, and take a few pictures. However, her morning was free, and she could concentrate on her investigation.

As usual, Elora followed the same protocol. She got out of the car near the professor's house and, with her camera and press pass visible, began taking pictures of the surrounding houses. She would stand in front of a window for a few seconds and take a picture, and within minutes people would gather around her to see what it was all about. Then a curious lady would approach her respectfully, and Elora would drop everything and give her undivided attention. The lady would feel flattered and start talking nonstop.

This time, however, things did not go as she had hoped. A very vocal lady appeared in front of her and began to question her harshly:

- May I ask what you're doing here, Miss?

- Yes, I'm from the press, and I'm here to do a story, Elora replied, extremely surprised. Of course, if I'm not disturbing anyone.

She had never experienced anything like this before, and the lady continued in the same tone:

- I know very well who you are, but what you don't know, Miss Journalist, is that you are not allowed to photograph our homes and children without our permission. What report are you doing, and when can we read it? It seems to me that you're roaming the streets without any report. Please delete the pictures of my house and children. You don't have my permission to take pictures of minors. I'm not kidding, I'm going to report you to the press, to your bosses, I'm going to tell them that you're wandering around and disturbing the peace of the neighborhood. This is a person's private life. How dare you?

Elora felt a moment of panic. The crowd that had gathered around her no longer looked at her with sympathy, but rather with discontent. The people were emboldened by the attitude of the extremely vocal woman who had put her in her place and seemed unwilling to back down. It was a mistake to continue like this. Elora couldn't come up with a subject for a story, because this woman seemed to know exactly how to present the issue; she was even able to call the newspaper and ask the editor-in-chief or even the news director. Of course, they would cover her story, but she didn't want to be in the position of having to explain herself when she got back to the office.

So, it was with her tail between her legs that Elora headed back to her car. Her years of experience in the press had taught her that there were no doors she couldn't open. She drove around the neighborhood two or three times, finally stopping a few doors down from Liam Sharp's house. She wanted to make sure she didn't run into the woman she felt so intimidated by. There was something about this woman that unsettled Elora and took away the confidence she had built up over the years.

Elora knew how to talk to anyone, how to get what she wanted by persuasion, and when that didn't work, she even knew how to manipulate and get what she wanted. But this time, she felt like a child who had made a mistake and was being corrected by an adult. This feeling was really weird! She didn't want to experience it again. Still thinking about these things, she found herself standing in front of Liam Sharp's house. It was an understatement to call it a house; it was a full-fledged mansion, a mixture of opulence and good taste. And because the universe was on her side, and just when things were going badly, the law of synchronicity showed her that she was still on the right track, there in front of her, just a few steps away, was Liam Sharp, the professor who cheated at the game.

- Good afternoon, don't mind me, I'm doing a report on a bocce championship, could you guide me, if it's not too much to ask? After her encounter with the fierce lady, Elora used all her skills to find the most appropriate words in front of the professor.

- Good day, Mrs. Journalist, I'm a big fan of yours, I follow your articles with interest. I've been walking and I think we're going in the same direction. I can join you if you'd like.

- Of course, maybe you can tell me something about the neighborhood, which seems quiet and charming.

The two began to walk, and Liam gave her a complete presentation of the neighborhood with precise details. They walked more than half the way, and Elora began to change her mind about Liam. He was a polite young man, extremely attentive to every gesture and word. She realized that she felt very comfortable in his presence, and he was charming.

- What is your profession, Mr. Liam? Elora inquired, partly out of journalistic curiosity and partly out of a desire to learn more about the young man. Judging by the way you speak, I feel like a student in the front row. Let me guess, you're a teacher at a local school.

- You guessed half right, Miss Elora. Yes, I teach history, but I'm an assistant at the university. I'm a Ph.D. student in ancient mythology, and most of the time I'm busy teaching my students, working on my dissertation, and traveling. I've been to Greece six times for research. What little free time I have I spend walking or reading.

It was strange; Elora was very good with people, having read and studied books on body language and micro gestures. It was truly her passion to observe people's reactions to certain stimuli, to find out if she was being lied to or misled by her interlocutor. This young man, however, was downright sincere. This also explained why she couldn't find a teacher with his name at any school; he only taught at the university.

They both arrived at the park and Liam gave her a brief history of the sport called bocce. It was first played in ancient Egypt; then the sport reached the Greeks and Romans. During the Renaissance, the game made its way to Italy, from where it spread around the world.

- I see you're passionate about this game.

- I wouldn't call it a passion, but I do play occasionally. It reminds me of my childhood. I used to play with my parents in Boston, where I lived for a while. Now I live with my aunt Clara, who helps and supports me, also financially, during my doctorate. I like to come and watch those who play when I have time. It's usually older people who take the game very seriously. Today there is a championship and it's wonderful that you decided to write an article. I know their president personally; look, he's right in front of us.

Elora was genuinely pleased with how things had turned out. The dream couldn't be real. This young man had nothing in common with the Liam Sharp who would cheat to win a hockey game.

The interview with the bocce club president went very well and she thought it would make an excellent article. Liam had agreed to film her while she tried to play a game. It was a great atmosphere, and at the end Liam asked her out for coffee.

They sat on a charming patio, sipping highly aromatic coffee, laughing and enjoying each other's company.

- Please call me Liam. The young man surprised Elora. He seemed rather shy, but it turned out that he knew how to take the initiative. The journalist felt wooed by the young man, and after a very long time, she felt her hardened heart soften.

- Please call me Elora, and they both laughed.

What a strange and yet so real dream! But Liam was more than a dream; he was everything a woman could wish for in a man: sensitivity, seriousness and a lot of common sense.

- Do you like hockey? Elora found herself asking in a last attempt to make sure the dream wasn't something that was going to happen in a few days.

- Not at all. I played with friends in Boston when I was little, but I quickly lost interest. It seems like a pretty violent sport. I started playing badminton and got pretty good; I even won a local tournament when I was 12.

Elora relaxed and smiled; the young man before her was not the teacher she was looking for.

- My aunt is having a reception at seven. It would be my pleasure to invite you, but you will need to dress for dinner. It's a formal party. I must pick up my tuxedo from the cleaners.

- A party with tuxedos and evening gowns sounds interesting; maybe I'll come. Will you ask me out, Liam?

- If you want to call it that, it can be a date. Elora was surprised to see Liam blush like a teenager.

- Okay, you've convinced me. I must hurry and find an evening gown. See you at seven.

- I'll wait for you in front of the house where we met; I like to be on time. See you then.

The two young people shook hands in a friendly gesture, but each was hoping for a hug. Unexpectedly, feelings beyond simple friendship were beginning to emerge between them.

Elora stopped by the newsroom and guided by inspiration, posted the video of the bocce championship on her account and prepared the article, which she left for the editor-in-chief to review. She knew that Bonn would approve it, changing only a few words here and there. That was his style; he couldn't help it, but Elora knew it would be an article that would resonate with readers.

Back home, Elora spent more than two hours in front of the mirror, unable to find a dress that would do her justice. Liam would be wearing a tuxedo. Did they have a date? She was walking on shifting sands, and part of her was afraid to express her feelings, while another part was intrigued by the qualities she kept discovering in Liam.

At 6:45 p.m., she was outside the house of Liam's Aunt Clara. An imposing butler stood at the door, checking the guest list and paying his respects. Guests in elegant suits began to arrive from vintage rental cars. Elora expected to find the punctual Liam outside the house, but he was nowhere to be seen. She waited for 15 minutes and to her disappointment the young man didn't show up. I mean, if he had to pick her up from her house in a vintage car, she could understand the delay, but she was right in front of his house. All he had to do was come out and greet her. She walked nervously to the entrance and to her surprise, the butler found her name on the guest list. Well, at least he put her on the guest list. Maybe something came up and he couldn't make it; anything could happen. But it was already 19:25 and Liam was nowhere to be found. Elora wasn't in the mood for a party.

- Miss Journalist, a pleasant voice said behind her, and when she turned around, Elora discovered a very friendly old lady who, from her demeanor, must be the hostess of the party.

- Good evening, I'm looking for Liam, Mr. Sharp.

- Yes, he told me something about you today; you probably want to interview him. Where is this boy? It's not like him to be late. Wait a minute. I'll go to his apartment and bring him to you right away.

After another 20 minutes, Elora saw Liam climbing the stairs to the party room, looking around as if he was entering the house for the first time. All her senses were activated, and her inner state was a cocktail of irritation, disappointment and curiosity. She hopes he had a good enough explanation for not waiting for her! Elora approached him and Aunt Clara introduced them. Liam looked at her as if she were a stranger. What had happened to the young man she met a few hours ago, who was so different from this one?

- Pleased to meet you. I don't read much of the press, but
I've heard about you and I'm glad to finally meet you. Liam
Sharp is my name.

"Was that a joke or what? Just a few hours ago, this guy invited me
to his aunt's party and put me on the guest list. A few hours ago, he
shook my hand warmly and looked me in the eye, and now he's acting
like I'm a stranger?" Elora wondered.

Elora started to ask him about his profession, but Liam had a
block, as if he had landed from another world. Fortunately, Aunt Clara
stepped in and saved him by reminding him that he was a graduate student in Ancient Mythology.

The whole situation was slowly but surely becoming unbearable for
Elora. Not only had she not received the expected apology for waiting
outside the house as promised, but she was also being ignored by this
Liam.

"Is it possible to have a twin brother?" the journalist thought for a
moment. During lunch, Elora had noticed a birthmark on the young
man's neck. As an investigative journalist, she paid attention to all sorts
of specific details. But the mark was there, so the Liam of now and the
Liam of a few hours ago were one and the same person. Elora was furious! She was about to fall in love with someone who had showered
her with compliments in the morning and was now completely ignoring her!

Elora strategically positioned herself near him and engaged in
mundane conversations with various people. However, she was constantly aware of the young man's somewhat hostile behavior. Liam tried
to approach her, but his gestures were awkward; she didn't make it
any easier by leaving the group she was talking to just before Liam approached to talk to her.

The party wasn't large, but she found a few acquaintances to chat
with - two former university classmates; one was an engineer, the other

was involved in art sales. She easily steered the conversation to hockey, and when Liam approached her group, Elora asked her two friends a key question:

- Let's consider a hypothesis that may seem downright impossible. Imagine, gentlemen, that a team of these two trailed in the first two periods, but then the backup goalie tied the game in the final period and then scored the goals that won the game. A mere reserve goalkeeper changes the fate of an entire team!"

The former university colleague, the engineer and aficionado of probabilistic calculations, didn't wait a second to answer:

- Something like that, dear Elora, if it has a chance of happening, it's a chance of 1 in 14 million. It's practically impossible for something like that to happen!"

But the surprise came only now: Liam Sharp collapsed on a sofa. His body language betrayed him - her words had triggered this nervous state. From the corner of her eye, Elora saw his hands trembling. This was the Professor she had been looking for. So, the dream was true, even if it hadn't happened yet. But if the dream hadn't happened, how did this other Liam, or Fake Liam, know about it and react so strangely?

Liam abruptly left the party. He hurried down the stairs without saying goodbye to anyone. It was time to follow him. This character, this neighborhood schoolteacher, this impostor, had a secret that she wanted to uncover. Maybe the dream wasn't entirely true, but her subconscious had created it to warn her. How foolish she had been! She was on the verge of falling in love, letting her guard down after years of avoiding such feelings and dedicating herself to journalism precisely to avoid getting hurt! She was going to get revenge on this fake Liam and find out what had really happened to the polite and charming young man she had met that morning. The Ph.D. student with a passion for travel and bocce was not the schoolteacher with no manners and a passion for hockey, though she didn't know by what miracle they shared the same body!

Elora walked down the street and saw Liam enter the basement apartment. So, this was where the teacher lived. The apartment was lit, the window was open, and she could see and hear everything. The professor went into the bathroom and was talking to someone. Elora became more and more curious. Who could be in the bathroom of the teacher? The professor came out of the bathroom, picked up a blanket, and went back in, as if to cover someone. After a few minutes, he came out of the bathroom without the blanket, closed the window, and turned off the light. Who could he have been talking to, and why did he go into the bathroom with a blanket? Tomorrow was the day she would solve this mystery. For now, she had to sleep for a few hours and return disguised and with renewed strength to keep watch.

The Complaint

Liam woke up around six in the morning. He couldn't sleep and a thousand questions raced through his mind. First of all, everything seemed unbelievable. Aunt Clarinette's house had an extra floor, and it seemed to have been like that since 1928, when it was built; so, he was definitely in another universe.

He was a university assistant, teaching ancient mythology to students; this was further proof that his consciousness had landed here from a world of probably infinite universes.

Another incredible thing Liam experienced was that in this universe, things were delayed by two weeks, and the hockey game was scheduled for exactly 13 days later. So, Aunt Clarinette was going to Banff in a few days. But it was also possible that this universe had changed, and Aunt Clarinette was going somewhere else; or maybe she was staying home to throw another party; or maybe the goddess Athena, in her great wisdom, knew!

What Liam certainly remembered was entering the utility room with journalist Elora following him, ready to expose him when the three Squirrels players locked him in the room. He heard a noise and screamed when he saw Pillo, who in turn got scared and hit him with his beak on his hockey helmet. The more Liam thought about it, the more he realized that this moment seemed to be when his consciousness shifted to this universe. But when he woke up, he was still wearing the hockey gear, so it wasn't just a simple transfer of consciousness. It was extremely strange, and Liam couldn't understand it. On the other hand, Liam from this universe should have been in the hockey arena, probably in the same room with him, but what could a Ph.D. student be doing there? In this universe, there was no game that day, so there was no reason for him to accidentally go to a hockey arena where nothing was happening.

Another question mark was the fact that journalist Elora knew about the game, even though in this universe the game was scheduled to take place in two weeks. Elora recounted the match at the party with quite a few details, and she did it in such a way that he could hear her as she was narrating the match. To Liam, it seemed like some kind of declaration: "See, I know everything!" Where did this journalist get this information? Is she also a traveler through universes?

On the other hand, Pillo is also incredible. As a professor and history enthusiast, Liam could connect Pillo's appearance to certain myths and legends. He could think of the Phoenix bird, although Pillo was far from the description of that bird, and that bird was reborn from its own ashes. However, Pillo had the appearance of a few days old chick; perhaps when he grows and develops, he will be able to transform into a Phoenix bird. Although there were very few chances for Pillo to be the Phoenix Bird, he was certainly a crucial figure in this whole story.

In Norse mythology, two giant birds, Hræsvelgr and Veðrfölnir, lived at the top of the tree Yggdrasil, and when they flapped their wings, they created the wind that carried the Vikings far and wide in their explorations and battles.

Among the Egyptians, Liam found a giant bird named Bennu, who was none other than the god Ra.

In his studies, Liam had come across some information about giant birds in Native American culture, where these birds were the rulers of the sky and lightning.

But Pillo reminded Liam of a childhood game in which giant chicks attacked the planet and bombarded it with eggs. The player, on a cosmic ship, had to shoot and destroy these birds, occasionally coming up against a giant bird, a boss.

- Are you a boss that came to conquer the planet, Pillo? Liam asked, but the giant chick was sleeping peacefully in the bathtub.

So, a series of unanswered questions for Liam. He opened his laptop and began to search for information, more and more information that he didn't know. For a moment, Liam stopped and marveled at the fact that the laptop was open and functional. This laptop had a password, which he entered without hesitation, and it worked! It seems that the two Liams mostly thought alike and chose the same password in different universes.

While checking his email, he had received several messages from students with their assignments, he received an email. It was from an address with a series of random letters and numbers. "Probably spam," Liam thought, but the subject was Pillo's name. Who could send him an email with the subject Pillo at 6 in the morning?

With disbelief and curiosity, Liam opened the email and read: "You have exactly three days to bring me the chick! Signed Q."

After a few moments of thought, Liam replied to the email: "Who are you and what do you want from me?"

Within seconds, he received a new email. "I just want you to bring me the chick willingly! Make no mistake, you are just a pawn on my chessboard!"

"That sounds like a threat," Liam thought. Someone wanted Pillo, and that someone knew that Pillo was with him. "Who are you, Q?"

"If you want to know my name, it is in front of your eyes, on all the grapes of Dionysus, little teacher!" the mysterious Q replied again.

Liam was speechless. This mysterious character who called himself Q seemed to know more about him than he first thought. He even used an expression he could use. Maybe he would have used another expression, like the stars crying in the night sky, Oh Uranus! but this character hit him pretty good with Dionysus.

The name of the person who was sending messages so early was in front of his eyes? There was a laptop in front of his eyes. Everything was so strange! The name of the person who had just threatened him and compared him to a pawn on his chessboard was Laptop? Qlaptop? This Qlaptop called him "Little Teacher", so there was a good chance that it knew he came from an alternate universe where he was a history teacher at the local school.

Liam left the laptop and sat on the bed, overwhelmed by so many unanswered questions. Whoever this Qlaptop character was, he had no intention of leaving Pillo. Liam had the impression that this giant chick would play an extremely important role in the coming hours and days. Maybe it was no coincidence that Liam ended up in this universe where everything happens two weeks earlier. Maybe he has to do something or fix something and needs Pillo's help; that seemed to be the most logical explanation, if we can talk about logic after everything that happened.

However, Liam had to be careful: on the one hand he saw the journalist as a threat, on the other hand this new character who had just approached him was a big fan of strategies and chess games. With these thoughts, Liam fell into a state of drowsiness. He planned to sleep as much as possible, wake up, and then go to an excellent restaurant to eat and enjoy the day, but his plan was quickly shattered.

Some horrible noises coming from the bathroom snapped Liam out of bed in an instant. He was on his feet, running around the room, disoriented and having no idea what had happened. In the bathroom, Pillo had become agitated and knocked over the shelf in front of the mirror, breaking the porcelain cup Liam kept his toothbrush in. It was this cup that he had... actually, this was another universe; Liam had no idea where the porcelain cup came from!

- What happened, Pillo?

- Pillo, pi pi! exclaimed the giant chick, who was red-faced and very upset.

- Do you have to go to the bathroom? I'm sorry, but I can't let you use my bathroom. I'll take you out on the lawn and you can sort yourself out there while I pick up the pieces and whatever else you broke.

Pillo didn't wait a second and dashed out the door into the backyard. Liam grabbed a bucket and started picking up the pieces. As he cleaned up the mess Pillo had made, he thought he needed to change his toothbrush anyway; he couldn't use the same toothbrush as Liam who was in this universe. Theoretically, this body he was in had brushed his teeth with that toothbrush, but he hadn't brushed with that toothbrush, so it wasn't his toothbrush. As he was relieved to have finished cleaning the bathroom and was about to go out to see what Pillo was doing, Liam heard a heavy knock on his apartment door.

Liam opened the door to find two massive individuals standing in front of him:

- Mr. Liam Sharp?

- Yes, please, how can I help you?

- Please follow us into the backyard.

- But who are you?

- We're from Animal Protection. You've been reported.

- I've been reported?! By whom?

- That's not your concern. We're here to conduct an investigation into the presence of a giant chick in your home and yard.

Liam followed the two into the backyard, marveling at the fact that Pillo had just come out into the yard, and someone had already called Animal Protection.

Out in the yard, Liam looked around and spotted Pillo sitting quietly on the grass.

- Is this the giant chick?
- If you see another one, please let me know.
- You're very spiritual, sir!

A black, unmarked car was parked on the street, and the two men were holding a folder with many completed papers in which they were searching for something with great interest. Liam waited impassively to see what the complaint was about. Neighbors were already gathering around Mr. Sharp's yard.

- Liam, what's going on?

Turning to see who was speaking, the young man found himself face to face with Mrs. Ivy Johnson, a neighbor whom he had helped several times to go shopping because she didn't have a car and found it difficult to carry bags home. Many times, this lovely lady would invite him into her home, serve him tea or coffee, and they would chat for a few minutes. Liam assumed that Liam from this universe had done the same; it was quite possible that these things happened here as well. Mrs. Ivy was known as an advocate for women's rights, a dedicated environmentalist, and a volunteer for various organizations.

- I don't know, Mrs. Ivy, these gentlemen are from the American Society for the Prevention of Cruelty to Animals and are trying to investigate.

- Please leave the yard; we are on duty, and you are disturbing us, one of them replied brusquely.

- Well, I should leave Mr. Sharp's property, but you know, you're amusing! Liam, did they identify themselves?

- Yes, they told me they were from Animal Control, Liam replied naively.

- I'm not referring to what they told you, but what they showed you. Did you see any identification, a badge, or anything to prove the authority they claim to have?

- They didn't show me anything; they just arrived and asked me to go out into the yard.

- Please, ma'am, don't interfere with an ongoing investigation; do the right thing and leave.

- Yes, you are really serious. Well, I want to participate in this investigation, of course, if Mr. Sharp accepts me. And Mrs. Ivy turned to Liam, waiting for his approval.

- You have no authority to do that; please leave, said one of the men.

- Oh, but I do. I am Mr. Sharp's legal counsel. And turning back to Liam, she continued: Liam, I understand the law; this is not the first time I've dealt with such an investigation.

- Mrs. Johnson is my legal counsel, and I want her to stay, Liam told the unexpected visitors at his door, who were questioning him about Pillo, who by the way was sitting quietly on the grass.

- As you wish, the investigators replied bluntly.

- Now, gentlemen, please present your badges, as you should have done the first time you knocked on my client's door, Mrs. Ivy continued.

The two were indeed from Animal Control, at least that's what their IDs looked like, which Mrs. Ivy studied carefully.

- So, tell me, what is the problem or complaint?

- Well, we received a complaint that there is a giant chick in this building. Mr. Sharp is this your chick? the investigators asked, pointing at Pillo.

- Allow me to joke, I hope you're not thinking that Mr. Sharp is a bird! This is Mr. Sharp's pet, Mrs. Ivy replied, looking at Pillo with gentleness.

- Do you have any proof, a permit, or a document that confirms what Mrs. Johnson is saying?

- Gentlemen, you should know the law before you ask such a question. In the state of Georgia, where we are, individuals can own a chick as a pet. There is no need for a permit if Mr. Sharp keeps the chick indoors and has the knowledge to take care of such a chick.

- Well, I understand what you're saying, Mrs. Johnson, but the law refers to a chick of normal size, a few inches.

- Well, and this is still a chick, just a little larger; but if we shrink it mathematically, we get a chick of a few days, of normal size, Mrs. Ivy replied in a calm, didactic tone.

- You seem to be exaggerating! This chick needs to be taken to the vet and examined to make sure it's not sick or carrying various diseases. It needs to be fed properly and given the proper conditions and environment. This chick, even though it is giant, needs a heat lamp and a safe place, like any chick of a few days. In addition, it may disturb neighbors, make noise at night, and being such a large chick, may cause damage or harm to a child or smaller animals, such as cats or small dogs. Mr. Sharp, you must understand that you are fully responsible for both the safety of your chick and what it can destroy.

- Gentlemen, forget it! This chick is only temporarily in this house and yard; we will find a place to keep it while respecting all the rules. You can come back another time and check if all the conditions for its growth and safety are met.

- This time we will only give you a warning, but next time we will come with the van and take the chick away, you should know that.

The two men from Animal Control left as quickly as they had come. The curious people who had gathered around Liam's house began to disperse, and Mrs. Johnson whispered to Liam:

- We need to talk. Take the van from the university and go with the chicken to this address where you can leave Pillo safely. Then meet me at my place. I almost forgot: Here's my number. Call me when you get there so I can give you the access code to the building.

Liam remained speechless while Mrs. Ivy walked calmly to her home, as if nothing that had happened earlier had disturbed her day. Pillo, however, was happy; he stood up and began to walk gracefully through the yard. But as he stood up, Liam noticed that Pillo had been standing on a mound of dirt. The chick had dug a hole, pooped in it, and then covered it with dirt. It seemed like a civilized chick, but Liam couldn't keep it here because it would destroy the garden in a few days, and he couldn't keep it in the bathtub either, that was for sure.

Mrs. Johnson mentioned something about the university van; what was that about? He went out into the street, and there was no one there, only passersby who didn't pay any attention to him; the neighbors and curious onlookers had left a few minutes ago.

Looking left and right, there was indeed a car in front of the house, and it had the university logo on one side. So, in this universe, Liam was using a university car. That was good, because he couldn't take Pillo on the bike he used to travel around the neighborhood and taking him on the bus was out of the question, especially now that the animal control people had their eyes on him.

- Pillo, don't leave here, please be good and don't misbehave, you've seen them! If they come back, they'll take you with them!

- Piiii, piiii, said the giant chick, extremely nervous.

- That's right, those gentlemen want to take you away from me! We have to go somewhere to find a place to keep you. Mrs. Johnson, Mrs. Ivy, whom you saw earlier, has a plan; she's given me an address, and you'll stay there for a few hours until we find a permanent solution. Now I have to find the keys to this van. Stay quiet here! Promise to be good?

- Looooo, Looo, Pillo replied and sat down quietly on the grass.

Liam breathed a sigh of relief. At least he solved one problem! But where were the keys? He entered the apartment, but there were only crumbs from Pillo's dinner on the floor, and everything was a mess. If Animal Control hadn't come and forced him to take the chick out of the apartment, he would have had to find a solution himself, because he couldn't keep Pillo in that small apartment.

Finally, he found the documents, keys and savings from this universe hidden in the same place where he kept his savings. It seems that his double in this universe was much more calculating and had over 5000 dollars saved. This was normal; after all, the salary from the university was higher than his simple salary as a neighborhood teacher! He didn't feel the slightest guilt and took the money without remorse. Pillo's life was the most important thing right now! Liam couldn't afford to lose him or let him fall into the hands of bad people like the Qlaptop who had written to him that morning. May Hestia, the goddess of home and hearth, bless the path and find a shelter for Pillo full of warmth, safety, and hospitality.

As he left the house, the little one was waiting in front of the van. Liam opened the back and Pillo happily got in because there was enough room, and he didn't feel crowded. Liam wanted to make sure that Pillo was safe, so he climbed into the van. There were some hoodies that the students used when they went to sports competitions. Looking for the biggest one, he dressed Pillo in one, and Pillo seemed very excited. Satisfied with the idea of dressing Pillo, Liam got behind the wheel and as he was about to drive away, he saw Aunt Clarinette getting out of a taxi. But it seemed no one in this universe called her that, so he had to be careful what he said.

- What are you doing, Liam, you said you weren't going to the university today.

- I got called in to help someone with an anthrozoological study.

- What kind of science is that, and what do you have to do with zoology?

- Well, Aunt Clara, as far as I know, it's an academic discipline, and as far as I'm concerned, the study has to do with myths and legends about giant animals.

- Like dragons and stuff?

- No! It's about giant birds; I'll tell you more when I get back from the university.

- Good. When you come back, please come see me, because I'll leave you some instructions. I hope you haven't forgotten I'm going to Banff!

So, Aunt Clarinette in this universe doesn't miss the vacation in Banff and the trips with her friends of the same age. Things are beginning to resemble some of what he knew. Aunt Clarinette was walking to the front door when she turned and scolded Liam:

- Oh, and you should know that you were not very nice to that journalist! You left without talking to her, and she, poor thing, left the party right after you, probably upset.

Liam waved to his aunt and left in the university van, thinking about the journalist. Well, she left right after him, so there's a good chance she went down and saw him from the street with Pillo, and she probably called Animal Control. But that seemed impossible because the little one was sleeping in the bathtub when he entered the apartment. This means that someone else reported him to the animal shelter, most likely the strategic gaming enthusiast Qlaptop! It seems he would do anything to get his hands on Pillo!

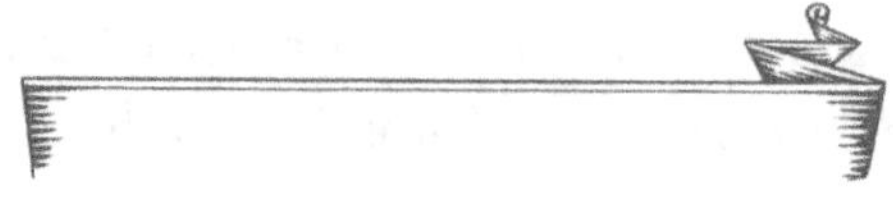

The Assassins

Elora slept little, dreaming of something confusing, but she couldn't remember what it was. Perhaps it would have been better to dream something that would show her what she would do today. She needed information because something unimaginable had happened. The young man she had met yesterday, who had been absolutely charming, a polite and educated young man, had nothing in common with the Liam Sharp she had met at the party.

At that moment, her journalist's mind began to speculate: maybe there's a device, the latest invention of scientists. Or maybe they found this technology buried in an underground temple, and certain individuals are using it on people, changing their thoughts and personalities. But who would want to use such technology on a university assistant? There must be another explanation.

It was morning, and the only sound was that of the refrigerator. In the quiet of the early day, Elora managed to detect a strange sound in the house: it was like a whirring coming from the entrance hall. Frightened, she jumped out of bed, holding her small talisman, a black stone on a gold chain. The stone had been given to her by an old shaman of the Aetas tribe whom she'd visited near Mount Pinatubo, where there is also a volcano. The shaman told her that he had found the stone in a volcanic rock in Lake Pinatubo. Elora had come to the Philippines to write a story about this lake, considered sacred by the locals, with its green-blue waters and a view of unparalleled beauty. When she saw the lake, her first temptation was to dive into its waters, which she considered extremely pure, but the local guide told her it was dangerous due to possible toxic gas emissions in the area. However, the old shaman knew when it was safe to dive, and he told her the story of finding the rock, taking it home, and discovering the black stone inside, a 3 cm pearl-like black stone.

"It came from another world, and the volcano threw it into this one." Elora found the explanation strange, but she accepted the gift because the old shaman told her it would protect her as long as she wore it. The guide told her not to pay attention to the old man: "Miss, don't believe everything he says; he thinks he's a shaman and gives all the tourists such a stone, probably picked from the mountain slope." But with her childlike soul, Elora believed the shaman's story with all her heart.

With her hand on the talisman, Elora approached the hall and found an envelope slipped under the door. It took her only a second to recognize the shape of the envelope. The Source was no longer leaving the envelope for Mr. Collins. She thought that if she rushed to the window, she might be able to see who was leaving the building, but her curiosity disappeared very quickly when she remembered that the person behind these mysterious letters had ways of knowing if Elora was watching or not. Elora was very sure that she didn't want to lose The Source's trust.

"Keep an eye on Professor Sharp and his giant chick!" Signed Q.

- Oh my God, what is this? Elora screamed.

If she didn't know that The Source always delivered accurate information, Elora would have thought this was a bad joke. What giant chick was being referred to?

It was just a way to get to the truth. Each time she faced a more challenging case, Elora resorted to the most outrageous disguises. This time, she had to be even more creative in choosing her disguise, especially since Liam Sharp knew her now.

She dressed in boy's clothes, and with her slender body, she could pass for a teenager who had grown rapidly in the past few months. She tied her hair back and put on a wig that made her hair look messy; she wore a cap and sunglasses. Behind the building was parked the car she used for investigations: a van with the logo of a company that provided furniture transportation for people who were moving. The van was filled with furniture she used as props, collected from street corners where people discarded them. She took her binoculars and put on a blue jumpsuit over her boyish clothes, fastened with snaps that she could get rid of in seconds if she wanted to, and unbuttoned it immediately.

- I'm ready to follow Professor Sharp around the clock until I discover his secret, Elora encouraged herself again, aloud, accustomed to organizing her thoughts this way.

It was almost nine o'clock when the moving van pulled up across the street from Liam Sharp's house. Elora had easily found a free parking space until 3 p.m. and hoped not to have to stay until then. The small refrigerator in the van was filled with cold juices and sandwiches from the supermarket. They weren't the best, but under the circumstances she couldn't have high expectations. She plugged in her laptop and, with nothing happening outside, began to search for more information on Liam Sharp. After several unsuccessful attempts, she felt frustrated; apart from papers published in academic journals, there wasn't much on the Internet about the professor. She probably wanted to hire a detective or a digital research professional, not to mention a hacker. It wasn't the first time she'd done this, and she had the name of someone in mind who could do it very well and discreetly, for a considerable sum of money, of course.

The phone rang, and it was someone from the newsroom:

- Elora, there's no need to come to work today; there's a power outage in the building, and it will last until the afternoon.

The newsroom had a generator that kicked in in such situations. The management had prepared general articles to fill the pages of the newspaper, which had to be published every day, no matter what. Elora had to write two such articles every month, and since there hadn't been any emergencies in the last few months, the editor-in-chief could choose one of the articles she had written in the past. This meant that she could concentrate on tracking without any worries.

Nothing foreshadowed what Elora was about to see! The street was quiet, and besides her car, only a few pedestrians passed by, either running or strolling. She looked towards the courtyard and Liam Sharp's ground-floor apartment when suddenly the door opened, and a huge chick rushed out. At first, she thought it was a person in a mascot costume, like those at basketball or hockey games. But the chick ran into the courtyard and dug a hole in the grass; it looked like it had to go to the bathroom.

What Elora saw was pure madness! In her entire career as a journalist, she had never seen anything like it! And she didn't even believe that such a gigantic chick could exist. For a moment, she thought about getting out of the car and seeing the chick up close. The chick seemed happy; it had covered the hole with dirt and was calmly sitting on it. She congratulated herself for not getting out of the car, because next to the passenger door, two very strange people were talking in a whisper near her van, without noticing her presence:

- You knock on the door, check if the gun is loaded, and be ready! The boss told us to solve the problem as soon as possible, said one of them.

They were two massive individuals who had parked their car behind the van and were now making their way to Liam Sharp's house.

They resembled bodyguards or bodybuilders, as the muscles under their suits were well defined. They walked swaying, a sign that they didn't feel very comfortable dressed like that. The two were armed, and their intentions were certainly not peaceful. The journalist decided to stay behind the wheel, and if the two became violent, she would honk to draw their attention.

Elora left the window open so she could hear the conversation that was taking place in the yard. Liam Sharp had come out, and the two introduced themselves as animal rights activists.

At one point, a middle-aged woman approached Liam Sharp's yard from the crowd of passersby who had stopped to see what was happening in their quiet neighborhood. It took Elora only a split second to recognize the woman who had forced her to leave from the front of her home just yesterday morning. It was the lady in whose presence she felt uneasy. This lady seemed to be everywhere, interfering with everyone. Now she had become Liam's attorney.

After a few minutes of discussion, the two so-called animal control officers left. But even though they got into their car and drove off in a hurry, Elora saw them return to the street a few minutes later, stopping the car a few houses down. Liam Sharp, however, did not suspect anything; he loaded the huge chick into a van with university markings and spoke for a few seconds with his aunt, who was returning from the city in a taxi. Soon Liam drove off with the van and the chick to an unknown location.

A few seconds after Liam left, the two individuals, who looked like bodyguards and were not animal rights activists, started chasing the professor and the giant chick. It was going to be a double chase, with her following those who were following Liam Sharp. Elora could feel the adrenaline coursing through her veins, a sensation she had experienced before, but never as intensely as now!

After several minutes of driving towards the outskirts of the city, Liam stopped the university van in front of some warehouses. They were a type of warehouse that certain people rented to store various items that they considered valuable but no longer needed.

Liam made a phone call and probably got the access code to one of those warehouses. Elora couldn't see which one, though, because she kept a considerable distance between her van and the car of the two possible assassins, just in case.

Liam opened the warehouse, took the chicken out of the van he had come with, and left alone after a few more minutes. He probably thought he was leaving the chick safe for a few hours, but he was wrong! The two individuals got out of the car and walked slowly towards the warehouse Liam had come out of.

They probably intended to kidnap or kill the chick. What could she do? It was too late to call the police, they were on the outskirts of the city. Elora got out of the van and slowly approached the warehouse; she was disguised and felt in her element. She watched as the two tried to open the lock and finally succeeded. They seemed to be professionals, and most dangerous of all, they were armed.

The journalist in her overcame her fear and turned on the camera she had strapped to her shoulder, a small action camera capable of capturing high quality footage. Strange and piercing sounds came from inside, as if someone was crying. Maybe the chick was crying, Elora thought, peering cautiously through the slightly open door. The two assassins were laughing out loud. No one was crying. One of them was on his knees, leaning forward and pounding the floor with his palm, while the other was on his back, laughing and holding his stomach, making the whole warehouse shake. The giant chick moved around them, making strange noises: "Piiiiiii Llooooo, Piiiiiii Llooooo!" Hearing these sounds, the two laughed even harder, their faces turning red to the point of suffocation.

At that moment, Elora felt the talisman around her neck, given to her by the shaman from the Philippines, warm up and pulsate. She found nothing funny about the scene before her and thought that the talisman protected her. It didn't take her long to understand that she couldn't leave the chick with those two assassins. Without giving it much thought, Elora entered the warehouse and approached the chick:

- Come with me, little one, I won't hurt you. Trust me.
- Pillo! Pillo! said the chick and followed Elora.
- I am Elora, and I assume you are Pillo. Let's not waste any more time.

From behind, the two assassins could be heard laughing, but probably when the chick moved away from the warehouse, they would recover and notice her absence. Elora opened the van and put Pillo on one of the seats.

- Stay here quietly and don't worry; I may have to speed up, especially if those guys follow us.

- Loooo Loooo, the giant chick replied.

Elora started the engine and sped off. Behind her, the two assassins were already on the road, moving with difficulty, as if they were drunk and trembling from the exhausting laughter. But the danger had not passed, and Elora was aware of it. The two were professional killers and would probably follow them. Elora stepped on the gas and headed for the city center.

- You okay back there, Pillo?
- Looooo, looooo, she heard the chick scream in a guttural voice.

Where were they going to hide? Sure, she shouldn't have left the chick with those two assassins, but now she was caught in the middle and completely exposed. It wasn't wise to play with those two dangerous individuals!

The traffic became more and more difficult, and finally Elora parked the car on the side of the road, right next to a sign that said, "No Parking". She got out of the car, opened the back door, and helped Pillo, who was feeling a bit dizzy.

- We need to go where there are a lot of people, okay, Pillo? Those guys from the warehouse are following us, and I think they want to hurt you.

- Loooo, loooo, Pillo replied, and Elora took those sounds as a "yes".

They ran for more than ten minutes, and Pillo was breathing heavily and sweating profusely.

- Hang in there a little longer, buddy!

Elora felt relieved when she saw the multi-purpose hall in front of her, where various concerts, contests and competitions took place. There was a rock concert going on. All the while, she didn't turn her head to see the two assassins, but she could feel them behind her.

Arriving at the entrance, Elora had a stroke of genius.

- I'm with the concert mascot, please let me in; we need to get backstage.

- But we haven't been notified of your arrival. Please wait, replied one of the security guards.

- Sir, you don't understand. The mascot must go on stage now! Take us to the stage now!

The security guard stopped, as if something more powerful than him was commanding him. Elora wasn't aware of what she had done and the fact that she could influence the will of other people. The journalist was just happy to see the whole team moving towards the stage. She thought it was the safest place to be, because out of the corner of her eye she saw the two assassins approaching the concert venue. They were only a few seconds behind her!

The stage became the only safe place because the assassins couldn't reach it. Coincidentally, Elora and Pillo ended up on stage during a break when the artists went out to change their costumes. When Pillo appeared on stage, the concert hall fell into complete silence. Twenty thousand people couldn't understand why a slender young man and a mascot had climbed onto the stage. But Pillo, unknowingly, tripped over a cable and fell, rolling twice. The audience erupted in laughter, and encouraged by their attitude, Pillo slowly stood up, took the microphone, and began to sing.

- Piiiiii Lloooo, Piiiiiii Looooooo.

That was enough for the audience, who burst into uncontrollable laughter. It seemed that one of the powers of this giant chick was to make people laugh out loud. Thousands of people laughed so hard that the concert hall shook. Laughter was contagious, and even the most serious people in the room began to laugh from the bottom of their hearts.

Elora came to the microphone and said in a husky voice:

- You have met Pillo, the mascot of this concert.

To the applause of the audience, the two walked off the stage and into the hall. People cheered and made room for them in the crowd. Behind them, the rows closed so that no one could follow them, completely surrounded by laughing people. It was a brilliant strategy: people were convinced they had a mascot in front of them and enjoyed greeting Pillo.

Eventually, Elora managed to reach one of the service exits, leaving the hall pulsating with the rhythms of rock music. Once on the street, the two of them boarded the first bus that stopped at the station.

- Two tickets, please.

- You've been very funny, little one, said the driver, and the whole bus applauded Pillo.

It seemed that the rock concert idea had made the giant chick popular; in just a few minutes, he became a sensation on social media. The two traveled through several stations, and Elora got off at the end of the line. Pillo took lots of photos with his fans and the driver, who didn't let them off until the little one repeated the song from the stage. All the passengers burst out laughing, and the driver had to stop the bus for a few minutes until the laughter died down.

It was evening. The two walked down a dimly lit street. Elora breathed a sigh of relief when she saw that the two assassins were no longer following her. They stopped in front of a tall building that looked like a huge garage, with some apartments on the top floor, but the entire building was in total darkness.

- We have to open this door somehow, but it's made of metal, and I don't have the strength to push it open.

- Looo looo: that's what the giant chick needed, and when he bumped into the metal door, it opened immediately.

Elora only heard the sound of metal as the pieces of the door latch fell to the cement. They were now in an abandoned fire station. The idea had occurred to her just before boarding the bus. Where was she going to hide the little one? Then she remembered that she had written an article about this place and even interviewed the city officials when this fire station was closed. It seemed like the best place to hide a giant chick with two assassins in hot pursuit.

- Now it's time for me to go home, Elora said.

Pillo began to make sounds that would melt anyone's heart. Again, Elora felt her amulet warm and pulsate around her neck. It seemed to protect her from the influence Pillo had on humans. She realized that she hadn't burst out laughing in the warehouse, at the concert, and she hadn't been impressed by the endearing sounds Pillo made.

- Don't be afraid, little one, I'll come to you tomorrow. Stay here calmly until I come, understood?

- Looooo, looooo, Pillo made some sounds that Elora interpreted as gratitude.

Elora hugged Pillo and went out into the street. She wanted to clear her mind. She refused to leave immediately and sat down on the curb near the entrance of the abandoned fire station. She felt the need to review the entire day. In the morning, she parked the van near Liam's house and watched all the movements on the street. Around noon, the two assassins left after Liam Sharp, arrived at the warehouse in a few minutes, and from there she took Pillo, with whom they fled to the concert. They left the concert, boarded the bus, and got off in front of the fire station. According to her calculations, only an hour and a half had passed between leaving Liam's house and now. But now it was night. When did the time passed?

Elora got up and left the abandoned fire station. She had to find the van and make sure she wouldn't run into the guys from the morning until she got home. Pillo was probably asleep by now; she would return to him in the morning.

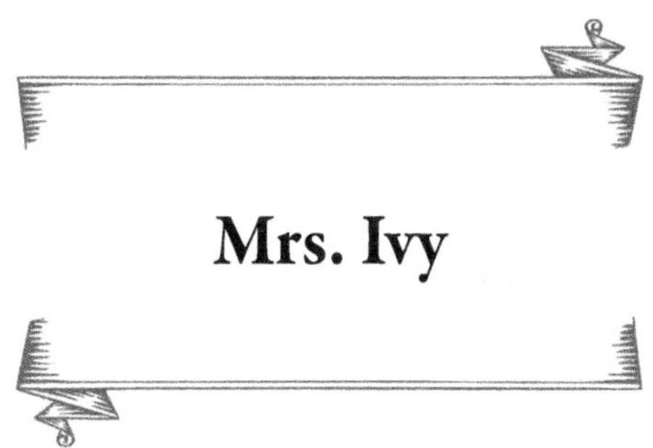

Mrs. Ivy

Pillo is safe. It seems Mrs. Ivy Johnson was a resourceful person. Liam would never have thought of the storage room to keep Pillo safe. His only concern was that the chick stays quiet and not attract any more attention. Liam had planned to stop by the warehouse later and leave some food and water for Pillo, especially since he knew how hungry the little one was. But for now, he had to talk to Mrs. Ivy as soon as possible and find a permanent solution to Pillo's situation. He couldn't keep the chick in the warehouse indefinitely.

Returning from the storeroom, Liam parked the car in front of Mrs. Ivy's house, in the same neighborhood, just two blocks from where he lived. The path to the house was filled with summer flowers that delighted the eye with their unique and fresh colors.

Liam knocked on the door and the woman opened it with a worried look on her face:

- Did you get the door open? Did the code work?

- Of course, but I have to go back in a few hours and see how he's doing. You don't know what he can do there, unsupervised!

- We'll both go back. Now go wash your hands and sit down at the table. I've prepared something for you to eat. When was the last time you ate?

Good question. Liam calculated that he hadn't eaten anything substantial for more than 24 hours because everything had happened so fast. He had barely managed to taste two goat cheese and honey sandwiches, a smoked salmon crostini, and a couple of miniature pastries at the party. Now he didn't know whether to consider what Liam Sharp of this universe had eaten. But Mrs. Ivy had a surprise for him: a full breakfast. On the table were about four well-made eggs Benedict, a large soufflé omelet, cottage cheese and avocado toast, a breakfast burrito, a giant glass of mango and banana smoothie, and five croissants with butter and lemon jam.

- Are these just for me? Liam asked, casting greedy glances at the carefully laid table.

- Eat, Liam, Mrs. Ivy replied gently. We don't know when or what you'll be eating for the next few hours. Eat until you feel full, then I will tell you everything I know.

Liam thought it was impossible for anyone to eat over 5000 calories, as much as the food on the table seemed to have. But everything tasted so good that the more he ate, the hungrier he became. He had long exceeded the limit of being overfed, so he stopped eating with a sigh and sat down in the chair, overwhelmed with emotion and fatigue.

- Dear Liam, you should know that you are not in the universe in which you were born and raised. Yesterday you made a leap into this universe, Mrs. Ivy said in a calm tone, as if what she was saying was perfectly normal.

- But how do you know that? Liam replied, confused.

- I'll explain everything, just be patient. Not only are you in another universe, but time here is shifted by two weeks, so we can say that you are also in another timeline.

- I noticed that too.

- So, something happened to you because of an extraordinary event in your universe, Mrs. Ivy continued.

- You mean Pillo, of course, Liam intervened.

- No. I mean Mr. Ward's skates.

- Do you know Mr. Ward? Liam said, increasingly astonished by Mrs. Ivy's words.

- Yes, I do. Mr. Ward is my ex-husband.

Liam didn't know what to say; it all seemed unbelievable. Ever since he had met Pillo in the utility room of the hockey arena, he had believed that the leap into another universe was due to Pillo. However, that didn't seem to be the case. Even though Mrs. Ivy was confident in her claims, Liam felt that there was a direct connection between Pillo's appearance, the leap to this universe, and this timeline.

- How do you think a backup goalie can score five goals and lead the team to victory?

- It seems you know about the hockey game too? Liam couldn't believe what he was hearing!

- I'd love to know more, but my knowledge is pretty limited. Look, I'll make you some coffee and explain. This world is made up of an infinite number of universes. Each of us has millions, if not billions, of duplicates. It may seem like a lot but think of the vast infinity and you'll understand. However, certain events change the predetermined order. Let's say we find one last pebble in a universe full of oceans, and this unique thing in the universe has extraordinary power. There are treasure hunters who go from universe to universe looking for such things, trying to collect as many unique things as they can. Look here: this bracelet is made up of 9 little stones that you might think I picked up from the flower garden, but that's not the case. Each stone is unique and comes from a different universe. This bracelet gives me the ability or the power to maintain the same consciousness in multiple universes. Mr. Ward's skates were the last ones in one universe, and their uniqueness opened the portal through which your consciousness came here. You crossed from your universe to this one, remembering everything that happened in your universe. Well, I can remember all the other universes to a small extent, but here's the catch: first, many of my memories are very vague, and second, my imagination can create certain scenarios that have no connection to reality. Do you understand?

- I'm trying to understand, Liam said, shifting uncomfortably in his chair. So, I should understand that there are people who move from one universe to another?

- No, no one can leave their universe and go to another where there is a double of themselves. Call it a paradox of identity or whatever you want. No universe can support two consciousnesses of the same person at the same time. For you to come here, Liam Sharp from this universe had to take your place in your universe. I, or well, my version from that universe, was waiting for that Liam outside the hockey arena, and together they're trying to elude the journalist who filmed you scoring all those goals.

- Well, in that universe he should have been near the hockey arena too, Liam intervened.

- Correct! I picked him up yesterday from the front of the house where he had a meeting with that annoying journalist and took him to the arena. That is where the consciousness exchange took place. Don't ask me too much about it, because I'm not an expert. I was waiting for you to come out of the utility room, and I would explain everything. I couldn't believe it when I saw you with the giant chick.

- By all the gods! What is Pillo's role in all this? How could he come from another universe?

- I don't know, and I've been thinking about it since yesterday. I searched for information in my memories and in the memories of other universes: absolutely nothing! I know that only certain objects can enter another universe in their physical form, but Pillo is not an object. That's why I didn't approach you last night, because I didn't know who this chick was, Mrs. Ivy confessed.

- Maybe it has to do with his state of consciousness, because he doesn't know how to say anything except "Pilloooo".

- Yes, there's something strange about him. But believe me, as far as I know, only certain objects, and usually small ones, can pass through a portal from one universe to another. The skates could be considered an exception. There are some people, like me, who have unique objects and who take or leave these unique pieces in one place or another. Those places are special and are gates of communication between universes. A simple glass marble that a child plays with can have extraordinary power because it comes from another universe where there is no other glass marble like it.

- So, there are people who look for these objects, or maybe even steal them, Liam thought aloud.

- Well, you're wrong, Liam. No one can steal such an object because it has no value to that person anymore. That object has to be bought or given by the person who owns it. All these stones on my bracelet were given to me by Mr. Ward, just like he gave you the skates. That's the only way you could feel this very strong energy and score so many goals; if you had stolen the skates, their power would have been nullified for you.

- Oh, Hermes, the great god of thieves! At least these unique items cannot be stolen. But I don't understand why Mr. Ward gave me the skates.

- My ex-husband is what you might call a treasure hunter. He has a certain knack for finding them. He goes to all the antique shops, flea markets, all kinds of stores. He tracks them down thinking he can sell them and get rich, and when he realizes they don't have any particular material value, he gives them away.

- He doesn't know about any of this? Liam wondered.

- I tried to talk to him about it, but he thought I was crazy. And when you think about it, for a person as grounded in reality as he is, all this can border on madness. But you should know that in other universes, Mr. Ward and I are still a couple, and we search for these objects together, and then we give them to those who need them.

- Interesting, Liam said. I think I understand what you're telling me, even if it's hard for me to accept. What really worries me is that someone wrote to me on my laptop this morning and asked me to give him Pillo.

- So, you found out about it too, replied the enigmatic Mrs. Ivy. How did the person who contacted you sign his name?

- He said he was forcing me to give up Pillo and signed Q and that the name was right in front of me. There was a laptop in front of me. Qlaptop?! I don't understand.

- Come on, it's not difficult, Mrs. Ivy encouraged him. If you have a laptop, what do you see when you look at it?

- The screen.

- Explore further; what do you see beyond it?

- The keys.

- Yes, here's the answer, you're very close.

- A combination of keys.

- Exactly! A combination beginning with the letter Q.

- Qwerty?

- What if it was a woman?

- Qwertya? Liam said hesitantly.

- Yes. She is the one who has collected dozens, if not hundreds, of such unique objects across many universes.

- She even knows who I am! She told me: Professor! So, she knows that I'm not from this universe. The question is, why does she want Pillo?

- I don't know. But the guys this morning who said they were from the animal rights group were her people. I intervened because they were armed and dangerous. They can't hurt you in my presence, at least I don't think so, Mrs. Ivy assured him.

Liam remained thoughtful. So, there's a person who has collected dozens of unique objects from different universes. How powerful is this Qwertya? Why did she want Pillo so badly? Is the little one safe there, alone in the warehouse?

- We can check on Pillo when you've finished eating. I've prepared two bags of food and some water bottles for him; I hope it's enough. Let's go, and Mrs. Ivy made her way to the front door.

Liam got into the car with Mrs. Ivy and started the engine, hoping that Pillo had waited patiently in the warehouse as he had asked him to do.

If the road to the warehouse was easier in the morning, now that it was afternoon, the two encountered a traffic jam and had to wait. As time passed, Liam's unease grew.

- Do you know anything about Pillo? Do you know if anything has happened to him?

- Dear Liam, things don't work like that. I don't see the future. I told you that my information is very limited, and I can't control the channel through which it reaches me. So, I can't have all the answers. When I start thinking about a particular problem, I start making things up, and that doesn't help. Sometimes I just don't know anything and I'm just as helpless as you are, Mrs. Ivy admitted.

Liam parked the car in front of the warehouse where he had left Tiny. The door was ajar, a sign that someone had forced it open. Who could it be?

- Let's go in and see what's in there, Mrs. Ivy.

Inside there was nothing, no trace of Pillo! Liam knelt as if after a strong emotion.

- I shouldn't have left him alone! What if he went somewhere and got lost? Liam blamed himself.

- How far could a giant chick go? But I'm afraid of something else. I should have thought that the guys from this morning might follow you, Mrs. Ivy regretted.

- We have no way of knowing if they took Pillo! Liam said disheartened.

- That's true, we have no way of knowing, and I didn't install surveillance cameras in this warehouse. I wanted it to be a discreet place, specially prepared for such situations.

Liam stood up and started to walk nervously through the warehouse when he suddenly kicked a metallic object.

- By the lightning of Zeus! What the hell is that?

- It's a gun, Mrs. Ivy said, a Glock 19 to be exact.

- Let's see if there's any blood, Liam got scared.

- There's no blood on the floor; I checked from the moment I saw that Pillo was no longer in the warehouse. But I found this feather.

- It's one of Pillo's feathers! Little one, are you okay?

Liam bent down and picked up the feather. But when he handed it to Mrs. Ivy, something extraordinary happened. The bracelet she was wearing warmed up, and a beam projected a three-dimensional hologram from it. In the hologram, the two saw Pillo and another person running toward the stage of a concert.

- What was that? exclaimed Liam in amazement.

- I have no idea what just happened! This is the first time I've ever seen anything like this. It seems that the giant chick's feather has the ability to activate these stones on my bracelet. But this is how we can find it.

- It seems unreal!

- What seems unreal to you? You just entered another universe, another time, and another body of your double. Don't you understand that we are just at the beginning of understanding, and in fact, we know very little about the grand infinity?

- Nevertheless, when I put the feather of a giant chicken near it, a hologram appears out of some stones, it's unreal! And on top of that, you see the chick in the hologram! How crazy does that sound?

- How crazy does it sound that a person who is the master of the seas and wields a trident can cause storms and earthquakes?

- Well, those are just legends, and Poseidon is a mythical figure, Liam said confidently.

- And why couldn't Pillo be such a character with abilities beyond our understanding? - Consider that the universe, according to the information we have, is over 13.5 billion years old. Anything is possible.

- Yes, but it's hard for me to believe that Pillo is anything but a mathematically scaled-up chick. If there are multiple universes, there could be chicks his size in a world where everything is scaled up in the same proportion. He seems to be what we think of as a chicken. Here such a chick is at most 10 centimeters. If we consider that Pillo is almost 2 meters, everything in the world he comes from is scaled up 20 times.

- I don't have any information, but I find it hard to believe.

- It seems more and more likely. You said that only small objects can pass from one dimension to another, like those stones on your bracelet. If we're talking about a gigantic world, then this chick is of small dimensions.

- But maybe Pillo comes from a universe where there are only giant chicks, and they are the dominant species.

- Let's check again where Pillo is. Give me the feather.

The two approached the feather on the bracelet again, but the hologram did not appear. The bracelet flickered twice, but nothing happened.

- It looks like we can't find Little anymore! Liam was discouraged. Maybe we need more feathers, Liam thought hopefully.

It was dark in the warehouse. Probably whoever had lost the weapon had turned off the electricity to surprise Pillo. Strangely, only one feather was left in the room. If there had been a fight, the warehouse would have looked completely different. In the light coming from outside through the open door, the room was barely visible; a strong light would be needed to see more details. Liam tried to use his phone's flashlight to look for more clues, but apart from the gun on the floor and the feather in his pocket, he found nothing.

- Let's go to the concert hall, Mrs. Ivy suggested. We're wasting time here. Let me call my network.

- Mrs. Ivy, I am at my wit's end! Do you have a network? What network are you talking about?

- My network of friends: it's the best network that gives me the most accurate information. We also have a group on a social network. I'll ask a question about the concerts in the city, and in a few minutes, we'll know everything, Mrs. Ivy confidently replied.

All the way to the concert hall, Liam could only think of Pillo; he was really worried about the little one's fate. What was the chick doing? Where was he? The hologram activated by his feather showed him running with a boy. Probably Pillo had somehow managed to confront the two assassins and was now trying to retreat to a crowded place; that seemed the most logical. But who was the young man with Pillo?

Suddenly, Mrs. Johnson interrupted his train of thought with news that shocked him:

- My network of friends has informed me that there is a rock concert in town, but it starts in four hours.

- Are you sure?

- More than sure. The person who confirmed the information is someone I trust completely.

- Oh, Hera, with your convoluted plans! exclaimed Liam. Was the hologram I saw on the bracelet nothing more than a projection of the future of where Pillo will be?

- Do you have any other explanation, Mr. Liam?

- I don't understand anything anymore! Just when I think I've finally figured something out in this mess, some new detail comes along and throws all my theories out the window!

- Welcome to my world, the world where people think Mrs. Johnson is crazy! Look, we're getting close. Try to park further away from the concert hall; you won't find any parking spaces nearby.

Much to his surprise, Liam found a large parking space and immediately pulled into it.

- Synchronicity! exclaimed Liam with satisfaction.

- What did you say? I didn't understand.

- Nothing, Mrs. Ivy. In fact, I was thinking that a parking space had just become available in front of us, and in less than five seconds, we had occupied that generous space, Liam explained.

- Maybe we'll be lucky enough to find Pillo safe and sound. I took the liberty of picking up the weapon that Qwertya's assassins had dropped.

- Oh, my goodness, Mrs. Johnson, I am totally against guns! Liam recoiled.

- So am I! Don't worry, we're safe. I accessed the memories of the other consciousnesses; you won't believe it, but the best thing to do at that moment was to take the gun with us! But don't worry, it's unloaded. I threw the bullets in a box of Vaseline in the warehouse; no one will find them there.

The two just had to wait for the hours to pass. A thousand questions ran through Liam's mind, but it seemed that Mrs. Ivy had decided to take a nap. He had no one to share all his thoughts and questions with. Liam felt a little tired too, but he was in a state of alertness, and even if he wanted to, he couldn't close his eyes! All he could do was hope that Pillo and the mysterious young man would show up soon.

The Fire Station

Liam began to worry. He had been in the car for over three hours and there was no sign of Pillo! And Mrs. Johnson was in the same state, sleeping peacefully. During all this time, thoughts had invaded his mind, and he realized that he needed more money. The savings of Liam, the university assistant, were not enough. It seemed that Qwertya was not joking when she sent assassins after Pillo, and Liam needed a place of his own to keep Pillo safe. That was the top priority.

At some point he thought he should wake Mrs. Ivy and make sure she was okay, but as long as she was breathing and her face was calm, Liam decided to let her rest. Maybe she was dreaming of something very beautiful, and he didn't want to be the one to interrupt her dream. He didn't know her very well, but maybe, with these unique stones from several universes, Mrs. Ivy was in a trance state, hypersensitive to outside stimuli.

His thoughts continued to wander to Mr. Ward and his skates. It all started with those skates; in fact, it all started with his desire to do something extraordinary that day. If he had found his skates, he wouldn't have gone to the sporting goods store, he wouldn't have been at Mr. Ward's house, he wouldn't have ended up at the hockey rink, and he wouldn't have found himself in this parallel universe. Still, Liam wasn't convinced; when something is meant to happen, it happens, one way or another. Maybe he would have found his new skates, gone to the arena, and there would have been the Squirrels team in the locker room, and the coach would have asked him to play instead of the backup goalie, but he would have discovered that his skates weren't sharpened, and then eventually someone would have given him those skates. So, no matter what, it had to happen that way.

It was very interesting that Mr. Ward was Mrs. Johnson's ex-husband. When Liam met Mr. Ward, he seemed to be a committed bachelor. He didn't say anything about his ex-wife and the story about the aunt was very strange. From what Mr. Ward said, this aunt was away in the mountains, but Liam felt that he was hiding or distorting the truth.

There was also Elora, with her filming the hockey game, which was watched by over two and a half million people. It seems that the other Liam has a hard time dealing with this overly curious journalist sticking her nose where it doesn't belong!

With plenty of time to waste, Liam started to remember how the journalist looked at him at the party last night. How did she know he wasn't the university assistant, and how did she know about the hockey game? One of the two guys the journalist was talking to said it was a one in a million chance. In fact, it's easier to win the lottery than for the backup goalie to win the game by scoring five goals.

In a second, Liam's face lit up. He knew where he could get the money: Mr. Ward's skates were the answer! Inside were the two messages from Violet and Rufus. Mr. Ward claimed that the numbers he hadn't played would have netted him more than $18 million! And since this universe was on a different timeline, Liam could still play those numbers. He got out of the car and ran to the nearest lottery store.

- You are lucky, the lottery clerk said. I was just about to close.

Liam bought a ticket and wrote down the numbers as he remembered them. Then he remembered that Mr. Ward wasn't sure if one number was 23 or 29, so Liam bought another ticket with the number 29, so he played the numbers 4, 25, 33, 23/29, 41, 44. Either way, he was going to win if those numbers were the winning numbers in that universe.

Liam returned to the car to find Mrs. Johnson impatient.

- Where have you been, what are you doing?

- I just stepped out for a moment because I felt like suffocating in the car; we've been sitting for hours and nothing's happening, Liam replied simply.

- Be patient, the concert is about to start. Please don't leave again and let me know what you want to do.

Liam, who had been open with Mrs. Ivy until that moment, found her last remark annoying. He didn't feel like telling Mrs. Ivy everything. After all, she wanted to help him, but Liam hated being told what he could and could not do! There was a good chance that the lottery numbers would win, if not this time, at least next time.

To be honest, analyzing the timeline in this universe, Mr. Ward might not even have gotten the skates. As far as Liam remembered, the skates were bought at a flea market. It was possible that Mr. Ward had bought the skates last Wednesday or would buy them later. Either way, he would think about it later.

More and more people approached the concert hall. Since nothing seemed to be happening, Liam and Mrs. Ivy decided to get out of the university van they had been waiting in for hours. But just as they were about to open the door, Pillo and the mysterious boy rushed past them.

- Did you see them? Mrs. Ivy asked impatiently.
- Let's follow them!

The chase proved difficult, with a sea of people between them and the chick. The huge chick, however, was easy to spot in the crowd because of its size and feathers. Still, no one was following it. Then why were they running so fast? Why were they in such a hurry? It was becoming increasingly difficult to move through the crowd on the way to the concert. At some point, they had to stop and wait for the sea of people to move. There was a traffic jam and tension was already in the air.

They entered a hall that could hold over 20 thousand spectators, and people were rushing to their seats, so it was normal for such crowds to form. Caught in the crowd, Liam noticed something yellow at his feet; at first, he was tempted to think it was packaging, but when he looked closer, he saw it was one of Pillo's feathers.

- I think we can track him; I found one of his feathers, Liam said, turning to Mrs. Ivy.

- Let's go back to the van and have a look.

- If we can make it through this crowd, Liam said.

- We'll make it. Follow me.

Taking Liam by the arm, Mrs. Ivy began to walk against the current through the crowd. It was a challenge at first, but when people saw her determined look, they moved aside. Eventually, the two of them reached the van.

- Let's see if we can use Pillo's feather.

As soon as Liam brought the feather close to the bracelet, it began to heat up, projecting the image of the giant chick into a dark room. Pillo walked calmly, and as he approached a brighter area, the two could see many fire extinguishers, shovels, picks, and fire hoses. It seemed as if Pillo were in a fire station. The image flickered and disappeared. The feather became useless at this point, but Liam carefully kept it in his pocket, next to the one he had found in the warehouse.

You never knew when one of Little One's feathers might come in handy.

- Did you see that, Liam? We know that our chick will be in a certain place in the future. It appears to be an abandoned fire station. Let me activate the friend network and we'll find out right away. Let's move away from the center as it will be blocked soon, and we don't know if we can get out.

Liam felt relieved because he had seen Pillo. He also liked the decision to leave the place because the crowd was exhausting. The two reached the car and drove to the edge of town.

Mrs. Ivy began to receive calls. The entire friend network had been activated, and in five minutes the two had the location of the abandoned fire station. Now all they had to do was get there.

They found the place easily, on a dimly lit street. Liam parked the van farther away and the two started walking, each one silent, lost in his thoughts. Less than 150 meters from where they parked the car, they easily found the empty fire station. Liam tried to open the door, but it was locked, and his burglary skills were non-existent.

- Come on Liam, let's see if there's a back entrance or a window we can use to get in.

Mrs. Ivy's idea wasn't a bad one after all. After several searches, they found a window they could force open and entered the headquarters. It was deserted; the fire station had been out of commission for months, and it was obvious that no one had been there since the last dedicated firefighters had locked the metal door and left with tears in their eyes. Budget cuts had affected them too; some had been transferred to other fire stations, and the older ones had probably retired. Now this headquarters sat unused, probably waiting to be turned into a luxurious residence. Surely, someone already had plans for this place, to renovate it and turn it into million-dollar homes.

"Speaking of which," Liam thought, "if I win the lottery, I'm going to buy this place; I'll have my bedroom upstairs, and downstairs I'll set up the whole room for Pillo. The little guy needs a big play area." But for now, Liam didn't know if the numbers he was playing in this universe were the right ones. Lost in his thoughts, he didn't even notice that Mrs. Ivy had disappeared from his field of vision. At some point he heard her calling him:

- Liam, come upstairs, go up the stairs and turn right.

Liam followed the instructions and found Mrs. Ivy in a former kitchen with only a few chairs and a table.

- This is where the firemen used to eat, talk or play all sorts of games. Let's get something to eat. Go to the bathroom and wash your hands; it's working, I checked. Come on, hurry up, Pillo could be here any minute.

Once again, Mrs. Johnson's tone irritated Liam and sent him to the bathroom like kindergarten kids. But he would have a more serious discussion with this slightly authoritarian lady later, after Pillo was safe. The irritation disappeared when he returned to find the table almost full of small sandwiches and some protein bars.

- But where did all this come from? Don't tell me the bracelet has such powers, oh Hephaestus, the mighty god of fire!

- I hate to disappoint you, dear Liam, but it's this bag that I carry with me like a boulder, and that I stuffed with food before I left home because I knew we'd have to wait. And we have to be as invisible as possible here; we can't just order food!

Liam realized he wasn't that hungry; the hearty breakfast he'd had that morning was more than enough. However, these snacks were perfect, especially if they had to wait in an empty building where he suspected there was no food. Mrs. Ivy seemed to be a resourceful person, even when it came to food.

It was getting dark outside, and the two waited in the dark in the former fire station.

- Have you heard anything? Mrs. Ivy asked Liam several times, but it was quiet outside.

After about 30 minutes, Liam heard a voice from outside that seemed familiar. They both got out of their seats and cautiously walked to the end of the stairs. From above and in the darkness, they could see the ground floor without being seen. They stopped at this strategic spot and waited. A muffled thud was heard and the two saw Pillo walk through the metal door. Behind him, holding a flashlight, was a boy who looked like a teenager, thin and disheveled. The voice, however, seemed to be that of a woman. Who was the person accompanying Pillo?

- It's the journalist, Mrs. Ivy said, as if she had read Liam's thoughts. Elora, and I don't know how, she added in a whisper.

- How did you figure it out? Liam found himself whispering.

- How? I noticed her yesterday morning when she was lurking around the neighborhood.

Elora was here too! Could she have had something to do with Pillo's departure from the warehouse where he had left him? This being was starting to get on Liam's nerves! Wherever he went, wherever he turned, he met her. For a moment, Liam thought she was nice, but he discovered that she was extremely annoying. This journalist was meddling in people's business: "She should mind her own business and leave me alone," the young man thought.

After less than three minutes at the fire station, Elora left, and Pillo sat down quietly on the floor, looking tired.

- Maybe he gets tired faster because he has such tiny legs and such a big body, Liam sympathized.

- Get the leftovers from the kitchen and let's go down to Tiny's, Mrs. Ivy whispered to him.

- Why are you still whispering? Liam replied in the same hushed tone.

- We have to make sure the journalist is gone. We need to feed Little. I have a bag of food for him in your van.

It seemed that Mrs. Johnson had an obsession with food, but on the other hand, she was right-Pillo had eaten almost nothing. He must have been very hungry.

The two of them stayed upstairs for a few minutes until they thought no one was around, and then they went down to see Pillo. He was overjoyed to see them. He rolled around on the floor for several minutes going "Loooo, Loooo".

The sandwich leftovers promptly disappeared, and Tiny seemed to have just developed an appetite.

- Let's get out of here, Mrs. Ivy said. Go and pull the van around the front; we'll come out after you turn off the headlights.

Again, Liam felt Mrs. Ivy ordering him around. He left with a heavy heart, especially because he saw Mrs. Ivy pick up the feathers that Pillo had left on the floor when he rolled like a happy dog, and those feathers were now in Mrs. Johnson's pocket.

Liam hurried to the van and then slowly pulled up to the front of the fire station. He turned off the headlights and rolled down the window. It was quiet and the sky was filled with extremely bright stars. He was tired and felt sleep creeping in, but he jerked awake when Pillo and Mrs. Ivy stopped in front of the car.

- Open the back quickly and put Pillo inside.

- Right now! Liam jumped out of the car and helped Tiny get into the van.

- Where are we going? Mrs. Ivy said in the same annoying tone. No wonder Mr. Ward lost his temper and left Mrs. Ivy; maybe she was a good person, but she didn't know how to talk nice, she only knew how to command.

- Anywhere, but not in the city. We're leaving the city. Do you know a place in the country where we can hide?

- No, I really don't know, Liam lamented.

- Okay, keep driving, keep going straight and be careful not to be followed. If you think there's a car behind us, pull over to the right and let it pass. It's time to activate the friend network and find a place to keep Tiny tonight.

Liam drove on, much calmer now that he knew Pillo was in the same car with him. He thought he should check his phone, which had been off for a couple of hours. When Mrs. Johnson had fallen asleep before the concert, Liam had turned off his phone so as not to wake her and because it was running out of battery. But he was sure that Aunt Clarinette, or well, Aunt Clara in this universe, was extremely upset with him. In the morning, she had specifically asked him to stop by to discuss her departure for Banff and to leave the house in his care. How was he going to apologize for not keeping his word? What would he tell her about his day?

- We're leaving town, Liam said, but Mrs. Ivy was focused on reading all the messages she was getting.

- Okay, okay, I think I found a place to stay tonight. Take Interstate I-75 North; we have to pass the Lookout Mountain Control Tower, it's about 190 kilometers, but we'll be safe there.

- So far? I don't even know if we have gas. We definitely need to refuel.

- There's a gas station on the right. Get in, fill up and let's go! Mrs. Ivy said.

Liam bought some gas and several bags of potato chips and a box of water from the gas station. He filled up and opened the back door where Pillo was eagerly waiting to eat. Tiny was extremely hungry and needed a proper dinner. He had Liam's money, the university assistant from this universe. A few thousand dollars would be enough. He wanted to order some big pizzas, but Mrs. Ivy was rushing him. Tiny would have to settle for the chips from the gas station, but Liam promised himself that he would treat him royally at the first opportunity. Pillo was extremely happy: he ate almost everything and then fell asleep in the back, overcome by fatigue.

The car drove through the night. Liam had completely given up on Mrs. Johnson's plan and could only hope that everything would work out in the end. The road was clear, and he hoped to reach his destination in less than two and a half hours. From there, he planned to call Aunt Clara in the morning and come up with the most incredible excuse. He still had time to think of something to get himself out of trouble. For almost an hour, everything went perfectly, only some infrastructure work caused a slight delay, but the traffic flowed smoothly.

At some point, the road ahead seemed to be blocked, with several cars in the middle of the road.

- Mrs. Ivy, I think there's a blockage ahead, forcing me to slow down.

- Good Lord! It's them, the guys from this morning. Turn the car around and let's take another route!

But it was too late! From behind the car came the sound of a helicopter.

- Oh, Zeus, with all your lightning, we're being chased by secret agents and a helicopter!

Liam cut the engine. Four agents approached from the front.

- Don't do anything stupid, Mrs. Ivy said. If it weren't for the helicopter, we might be able to distract them with the gun we took from the warehouse this morning, but there seem to be too many of them.

- I'm not the heroic type, don't worry, Liam said resignedly. What will they do with Pillo?

- I don't know, but stay calm, the game is not over yet. They used smoke grenades, I think.

Liam was astonished at Mrs. Ivy's reaction; what did she know beyond what could be seen with the naked eye? Qwertya's hired men were all around them. That many cars and a helicopter represented a significant deployment of forces, and those were not smoke grenades; it was most likely a sleeping gas, as the agents surrounding the car were wearing gas masks. From what he had read, Liam could swear it was chloroform or ethylene diamine. Seeing how much effort Qwertya put into catching him, Pillo must be extremely important!

Qwertya's Plan

Liam woke up and looked around; next to him were Pillo and Mrs. Johnson. All three were tied to chairs; but where were they? They seemed to be somewhere underground because there was no window in sight. Maybe they were in an underground base. Several agents walked past them, completely ignoring them. Each one seemed to have a role to play, and they were playing it with millimeter precision, almost robotically, Liam thought.

- Are you okay, little one?

- Piiiiii, Loooo, replied the giant chick with a voice that could melt your heart.

- Don't worry, little one, we'll get out of here, I promise, Mrs. Ivy's voice could be heard.

- I promise I won't leave you alone anymore and I'll protect you from now on, Liam added to calm Pillo down.

- You better not make promises you can't keep, Mr. Neighborhood School Teacher, a voice was heard.

Liam looked around puzzled, but the agents seemed to be concentrating on their real or imagined tasks. The voice came from somewhere else. Eventually, the young man discovered who was speaking: to their right was a giant screen. Who could be the creature with the voice distorted by an electronic device and wearing a black mask?

- I guess I have the honor to speak with the famous Qwertya, the young man said contemptuously; a great lover of strategies and games! The big boss of spies, assassins and secret agents, whose only business is to kidnap from the highway a neighborhood schoolteacher, a respected lady from the same neighborhood, and a gigantic chick! Without the three of us, you would be out of business, Mrs. Qwertya.

- Oh, Hera, keep me from taking revenge on this insolent individual! Did I say it right, the mythology enthusiast? Come on, tell me, a great fan of hockey games that you win alone in the last quarter as a backup goalie!

- Don't tell me you were at the game! Maybe you were even cheering for me at the last goal? Liam was surprised at himself; he felt in control, even though he was tied to the chair. He felt strong and capable of any comeback, which was quite unusual for a shy person who usually gets nervous in such situations.

- You'll be surprised to know that I was there.

- And didn't the universe implode? There can't be two Qwertyas in the same universe at the same time! Tell me, Mrs. Ivy, isn't that a space-time paradox or something?

- The paradox of multiple consciousness, Mrs. Johnson barked nervously, frustrated to be in this position, immobilized and forced to look in one direction at the screen where the voice was coming from. Would you have the decency to have your staff turn us around so we can see you, Madam Qwertya?

- You're both talking nonsense! If we're going to talk about a paradox, it's the paradox of unified consciousness. Yes, that's what I would call it. To be able to receive the consciousness of all your duplicates from all the universes in which they exist. And yes, one of my duplicates witnessed this game and I saw it as if I was there. Interesting, isn't it?

- Very interesting, I suppose you follow the Squirrels team and their sporting achievements with great interest! If you can afford a helicopter and a dozen agents, perhaps you could make a donation to our school's cheerleading squad, Liam quips.

- Liam Sharp, you are not ready to face my true power, the voice thundered, and the agents winced nervously.

- Oooo, Athena, give us the wisdom to stop angering the one who kidnapped us and tied us up in an underground lab, Liam shouted.

- Liam Sharp, you're eating out of my hand, and you don't even know it. You brought my giant chicken right where I wanted it! It was much harder for me to get it from the city; don't you realize that I'm always one step ahead of you?

- All I realize is that you're a freak, and no matter how multiverse you think you are, there are more complex things you need to be aware of. Don't worry, we're exactly where we need to be. We'll get through these agents quickly, and then we'll deal with you.

- Well, well, well! But this is a real threat! I am scared! I'm afraid you're not yourself; is the rope too tight? Shall I get the agents to loosen it a bit? You're pathetic! Now let's finish what we started!

- Piiiiii, Looooo, Piiiiii, Looooo! began Little, shaking and making these sounds, his head thrown back.

- No one is laughing, Pillo! What do you know, O Hermes, or whatever god you're referring to! We've taken precautions. Mr. Sharp, you may not know it, but your chicken has the power to make people laugh out loud. That's how it escaped from the warehouse where you left him. But my people carry a unique pebble from other universes and can no longer be influenced. It's time to start experimenting.

- Leave the chicken alone, what do you want with it? said Mrs. Ivy, squirming in her chair.

- This chicken, dear lady, is one of the strongest of its kind, and you won't believe it, but it has several unique abilities. If a mere pebble has powers, can you imagine what I can do with a living creature, a chick I can control? I've chased Pillo through several universes and each time he's managed to slip through my fingers, but now he's mine. I will train and control him as I please. Making you laugh out loud is just the tip of the iceberg; this chicken is resourceful!

Liam marvels that he's not laughing uproariously, as he should be without the protection of any rocks. If the agents laughed so hard this morning that they lost their guns, then something is wrong now. Then he felt Pillo's two feathers in his breast pocket. These feathers seemed to vibrate inside him. That might be an explanation. All the agents were wearing stones from other universes, Qwertya was either far away or she also had such an amulet, and Mrs. Ivy had the bracelet. He turned his head towards Mrs. Ivy and saw that the famous bracelet was no longer on her hand. Then why didn't she laugh out loud? Most likely, when Liam went to get the car in front of the fire station, Mrs. Johnson picked up at least one of Pillo's feathers from the ground as well. Suddenly he was jolted from his thoughts by Qwertya's distorted voice:

- I don't know the giant chicken's full powers, but having watched him for so long, I know his greatest weakness. Everyone, feed the chicken!

"What does that mean," Liam wondered, "what do you mean feed Pillo?"

- Are you trying to poison him? Little one, don't eat anything, Mrs. Ivy looked pleadingly at Pillo.

- You have understood nothing with your limited mind! I have no interest in poisoning it, I only need it for my next projects. But your chicken, as soon as it eats, it sleeps, and then you can do anything to it, it won't fight back.

Qwertya may be right: after emptying the fridge last night, Pillo fell asleep in the bathtub. And after eating the bags of chips in the van, he fell asleep again. But what could they do? How could they stop him from eating when Little Man was hungry all the time?

Pillo understood that he couldn't make the agents laugh and watched wide-eyed as they brought more and more food to the two tables in front of him. There were all the goodies: pizza, French fries, peanut butter and jelly sandwiches, popcorn, crackers, waffles, muffins, cookies, cupcakes, colored candy, ice cream, and soft drinks, enough to feed a battalion of 20 hungry kids after a day of play. His big eyes were shining, and Pillo's body could barely keep him from standing up and devouring the entire amount of food.

- Untie the beast and let him eat, Qwertya said in a mocking tone.

Two agents approached Pillo and untied his knots, and the little one shook himself a little and walked timidly toward the two tables.

- Pillo, don't eat, please! Hang in there, my friend, and I'll buy you more food. We'll open a pizza place or a hotdog bar, but please don't eat! Liam cried desperately.

- Kind of hard, neighborhood schoolteacher, to keep a giant chicken from eating what he likes best, Qwertya said, laughing with satisfaction. Come on, eat up, come on, food is waiting for you! Come on, boy, don't fail me. I am the emptiness that swallows all hope!

- Pillo, Aunt Ivy is making you 100 cakes later, Mrs. Ivy is also trying to get Pillo's attention from the tables full of food.

- That's a lot of cakes, Aunt Ivy, where do you bake them all? said the distorted voice again. Liam was sure he'd heard the same tone somewhere before, but he couldn't remember where.

- At my friends, if you're interested, Mrs. Qwertya. You'd be surprised how many people love Pillo!

- Yeah, especially since he's a star now that he's playing rock concerts.

But Liam and Mrs. Ivy had no idea of the adventures of Elora the Journalist and Little Man when he had the whole room rolling on the floor with laughter.

Meanwhile, the giant chicken took the first portion of sandwiches and devoured it immediately. Liam lowered his head; if Pillo were to fall asleep, Qwertya's plan could be carried through to completion, and the little one might become an object of observation in the laboratory of that evil being. He didn't even want to think about the experiments Qwertya could subject Little One to!

- Oh, Zeus, with your lightning and all, even you can't save this chicken! Am I right, Mr. Neighborhood School Teacher? the voice thunders.

- What are you going on and on about, Mr. Neighborhood School Teacher? Yeah, stop it, I get your joke, I laughed out loud, but now we can move on. You know, you're not funny at all, Liam said extremely frustrated. Let me tell you something. Believe it or not, in a few moments you're going to be desperate. You'll see for yourself, Madam Qwertya, and your despair is music to my ears! Your despair is my music! How good it sounds!

- Well said, Liam, Mrs. Ivy laughed.

- All right, Professor, you'll learn to respect me, no matter how long it takes, came the distorted voice with an intimidating tone.

- I understand. Then know that I will be a millstone around your neck. Or better yet, I have a more complex one that I'm telling you now: You're like a little bug to me, buzzing around and annoying me. But I can't help watching you, just to see what you're going to do next. What are you going to do if you lose this round? Liam continues defiantly.

- God, Liam, I didn't know you could be so funny, and Mrs. Ivy laughs uproariously.

- You laugh but look: your chicken has just finished its meal. What's the matter, baby, with that look on your face, I'm afraid you're not yourself. Are you sleepy?

No one would have expected the two tables full of food to be emptied so quickly by the chicken, which obviously hadn't eaten that well in a long time. All around were leftovers and bottles of drinks, which Pillo pinched the corks off and drank promptly.

- Come on, chicken, the agent will put you to bed now. Look how well you ate, bravo! Hmmm, interesting; yes, I think I won this round! Take the chicken, I think it's harmless.

Three or so agents approached Pillo, who seemed limp and about to fall asleep, but the moment they tried to grab him by the wings, the giant chicken became terribly angry, and a Piiiiiiiiiiiiiiii was heard, like a battle cry! The chick began to move extremely fast and hit the three of them on the head with its beak, knocking them unconscious on the ground. Liam knew the force of the blow, and luckily, he was wearing a hockey goalie helmet, but the agents didn't stand a chance against the giant chicken.

- Stop him! Qwertya yelled, alerting the agents.

But at that moment, Liam witnessed something he never thought he would see. Something extraordinary was happening. Pillo was moving with extraordinary speed; not only was he beating and knocking out all the agents, but in his rage, he was destroying all the equipment in the underground lab. At one point, Pillo tiredly stopped, walked over to the rest of the drink bottles, finished what was left, and threw the rest of the bottles on the floor.

- Thanks for the food, Liam laughed. Looks like Little enjoyed all the food, otherwise he wouldn't have had the energy to destroy the whole lab.

- You fools don't know who you're messing with! The lab door is locked from the outside, and I have the key. You're going to sit there and beg me to open it.

- Mrs. Qwertya, if I've learned anything from all your threats so far, it's that I shouldn't take them seriously.

- We will meet again, Liam Sharp. Oh, what a surprise I have in store for you!

- I don't think we've met yet, and please don't tell me your plans, I want to be surprised by your next move!

Annoyed by the voice on the screen, Pillo jumped and hit the screen with his beak, shattering it.

- Well done Little One, now come on and untie us, we need to find a way out of here.

Outside there was the sound of the helicopter taking off. It seemed that Qwertya had just left, full of resentment; the great laboratory was now completely destroyed. Pillo tugged on the strings, and they immediately snapped.

- Finally, we're free, Liam rose from his chair in satisfaction.

- Don't jump to conclusions. We need to find a way out of here. I'm worried about what Qwertya said, it looks like we're trapped in this underground lab with 10 unconscious agents. Let's take care of them, too. First we need to find my bracelet, in case Qwertya hasn't taken it. I'd hate to lose that bracelet. Second, we need the stones from other universes that the agents have with them, so we need to collect them quickly.

- You've thought this through, Mrs. Ivy. But why didn't Pillo fall asleep after lunch?

- Who knows, maybe his self-preservation instincts kicked in, he went into fight mode. Come on, stop talking and search the agents' pockets!

After a while...

- I've collected the ten stones, they're in my bag, but there's no sign of your bracelet, Liam said, eager to find a way out of the lab.

- Let's keep looking, Mrs. Ivy insisted.

The effort continued for another half hour, and finally the two found the bracelet on the floor. When Pillo destroyed the lab, it must have been in a desk drawer and fallen to the floor. Now there was no desk. The unconscious agents were lined up against the wall, handcuffed together, disarmed and no longer a threat.

- At last! Take a feather from Pillo and let's see where we have to go, said Mrs. Ivy, who always seemed to know what to do.

Liam picked up a feather from the giant chicken; there were dozens of them everywhere after all the trouble Pillo had caused. Liam put the feather on the bracelet, but nothing happened.

- Maybe we must wait a little longer, or maybe it only works when Little One is in danger, Liam said.

- But what's wrong with Little One? Why is he so restless?

Pillo was very restless and paced the room. Liam recognized the morning behavior.

- He wants to go to the toilet, he wants to get out, Liam understood.

- Sorry, Little One, but we can't get you out, we're stuck here.

- Piiiii, Loooo, replied the giant chicken and started for the metal door. He kicked it a few times, but the door didn't even move.

- We're stuck in here and I don't think any agent can help us even if he wakes up, we must find a solution!

- Wait, Pillo, look, me and Mrs. Ivy are thinking about how to get you out, just wait.

It was hard to tell a chicken with a physiological emergency to wait, and being a civilized chicken, Pillo didn't want to go to the bathroom until he was outside. That's when he started circling in the middle of the room.

- Maybe if he wiggles around like that, he'll calm down, Mrs. Johnson thought.

- I don't think so. I saw him this morning when he just couldn't take it anymore.

Pillo spun louder and louder, and in the middle of the room there was a little whirlwind that began to move the pieces of paper and feathers on the floor. The trumpet got bigger and louder, and Liam and Mrs. Ivy had to hold on to each other to keep their balance. Out of this mad whirl, Pillo suddenly broke free at full speed and hurled himself at the bunker door, which he smashed through.

- By all the gods of Olympus, if we've ever seen anything like it! Come on, Mrs. Ivy, let's have a look. I think the metal door had at least eight inches of metal and reinforcement.

From outside came the happy voice of Pillo, who had managed to solve his physiological emergency: Piiiii, loooooooooo.

The two were about to leave the lab when Liam stopped to look back again, more instinctively. The trumpet made of sheets, small objects and orange-yellow feathers fell silent, and in the middle of it the young man saw someone moving.

- There's a child, Mrs. Ivy, in the middle of the trumpet created by Pillo, Liam stammered in amazement.

- It looks like a child dressed in an astronaut suit. Who could that be? It was just us and the agents in the lab.

The two rushed over and managed to get the child's helmet off, but then they were completely surprised: there was no child in front of them, but a monkey.

- It's me, Violet, the Encyclopedia Monkey.

- Who? asked Liam and Mrs. Johnson in unison.

- I'm Pillo's traveling companion. I've come to help you. I've been stuck in another universe for two days; by the way, Liam Sharp, the university assistant, sends his regards. We had to clean up after your hockey game, and that reporter Elora gave us a big headache. Then there was Qwertya... we had a series of problems. Victory for Squirrels!!! shouted Violet the monkey as loud as she could! But if that was supposed to be funny, nobody was laughing.

Liam and Mrs. Ivy looked at each other quizzically. Who was Violet the Encyclopedia Monkey? Apparently, she had been trapped in the universe Liam had just left. They needed to get more explanations for all their questions, and since Pillo was unable to say anything except Pi and Lo, this Encyclopedia Monkey should be able to clear up all questions.

- But where is my little friend, Violet asked, looking around for Pillo.

- He went out, he had an emergency, he ate too much.

- Oh, poor little thing, Violet the monkey grimaced, I know what he's like at times like this. Let's get out of here as fast as we can!

- Where are we going? asked Mrs. Ivy.

- What timeline are we in?

- I don't know exactly what you mean, but what I've noticed is that time is two weeks behind the universe I left, Liam said.

- Interesting, said Violet the monkey. I have a question: In this universe, author Alexandra Aisling published a book called The Machinery Religion?

- I've never heard of such a book or author, said Mrs. Ivy.

- If she had published the book, you would have heard of her. So that's good, we can still beat Qwertya!

- What kind of machines are we talking about?

- The artificial intelligence that trained me. I come from a world of machinery, and Qwertya is collecting unique objects from many universes to control this universe. I'm part of a team that wants to stop her, and Qwertya will learn through suffering what it's like to mess with an encyclopedia monkey!

Liam looked wide-eyed at Mrs. Ivy, and they both stared in disbelief at the grand plans of a small, fragile, vulnerable being no bigger than a child!

www.ingramcontent.com/pod-product-compliance
Lightning Source LLC
Chambersburg PA
CBHW070406200726
48294CB00003B/1112